THE CASE OF THE
Daring Divorcee

Erle Stanley Gardner

THE CASE OF THE

Daring Divorcee

WALTER J. BLACK, INC., ROSLYN, N. Y.

THE CASE OF THE
Daring Divorcee

Perry Mason, having completed his luncheon conference, returned to his office to find a puzzled Della Street awaiting him.

"I tried to get you on the phone before you had left the restaurant," she said. "Your two-thirty appointment phoned to cancel, said that as soon as the other side knew Perry Mason was in the case the matter was satisfactorily adjusted. You are to send a bill."

"How much was involved?" Mason asked. "About five thousand dollars?"

"Six thousand, seven hundred and fifty was the amount of the settlement."

"Send a bill for five hundred dollars," Mason said. "What else is new, anything?"

"We have an office mystery."

"What do you mean?"

"This is a mystery that's right in the office. A woman apparently feels that her life is in danger and wants your protection, counsel and guidance. She also wants the help of a good private detective whom you are to select and supervise."

"Who is it?" Mason asked. "And where is she?"

"Her name is Adelle Hastings," Della said, "but your second question is one to which we don't have the answer."

Mason raised his eyebrows.

"I went to lunch at twelve-fifteen," Della said. "As you know, Gertie and I stagger the lunch hour. I grab a bite and am back by twelve-forty-five, then Gertie goes out and stays until one-thirty, while I keep an eye on the switchboard."

"Go ahead," Mason said.

"Well, you know Gertie. She's incurably romantic. If she ever pays any attention to a client she'll work up a whole story around that client. During the noon hour when there are very few calls coming in at the switchboard and people seldom call at the office, Gertie starts reading love stories and eating chocolate creams."

Mason grinned. "And then she tells me how she's watching her weight."

"Of course," Della said, smiling. "And she has now convinced herself that it's a scientific fact a little sweet before meals will kill her appetite and she won't eat so much. She says that our dietary habits are backwards, that we eat a meal and then eat a sweet; that we should eat a sweet and—"

"I know. I've heard Gertie expound her theories before. Let's get back to the mystery. You've aroused my interest."

"Well, Gertie was reading this love story. She had just come to the most interesting passage and I think she was reading with one eye and looking out for clients with the other.

"She said that within five minutes after I had left the office this woman came in and was terribly agitated. She said she had to see you right away.

"Gertie told her that you were out to lunch, that you seldom saw people without an appointment, that you might not be back before two-thirty, and that you had a two-thirty appointment.

"The woman was almost hysterical. She said, 'Never mind, never mind, I'll wait. He'll see me. I don't want to leave this office until I've arranged to have him protect me. I want Mr. Mason to look after my interests and I want him to get a good private detective.'"

"And then what?" Mason asked.

"Then Gertie asked her name and address and the woman gave the name of Mrs. Hastings and said her present address wasn't important.

"So Gertie wrote down the name and went back to her magazine reading. The woman sat down in that big chair by the window.

"After a few minutes the woman got up and started pacing the floor. Then she said, 'I'll be back in a minute or two,' opened the door and stepped out in the corridor."

"And then?" Mason asked.

"That's all," Della Street said. "She never came back."

"Oh well," Mason said, "she'll be showing up any minute now. What did she look like, Della?"

"Gertie was a little vague. She said that she had an aristocratic bearing, a good figure, a well-modulated voice and slender, tapering fingers. She thinks she was about thirty-two or thirty-three years old, but the woman was wearing huge dark glasses and Gertie couldn't tell very much about her features.

"Gertie told me that she was wearing the dark glasses because she had been crying. I asked her how she knew and she said, well, she thought the tone of the woman's voice indicated that she'd been crying. It had a sort of rasp to it."

"Leave it to Gertie," Mason said. "Aristocratic bearing, slender, tapering fingers, well-modulated voice— Do you suppose, Della, that by any chance Gertie has transposed the description of the heroine in the love story she was reading, to our client?"

"I wouldn't put it past her," Della said. "Gertie's usually pretty observing but during the noon hour when she's reading one of those love stories she's got her head way up in the pink clouds."

"Well," Mason said, looking at his watch, "we'll have time to do a little more work on these proposed instructions for the jury which I want to submit to the judge in the case that's coming up next week."

"There are a couple of very important letters which have been hanging fire," Della Street suggested. "They *should* go out today."

"All right." Mason sighed. "Get the letters. I know what that means, however. You'll bring in a stack of mail eighteen inches high, get the two urgent letters off the top and then tell me I really should run through the rest of the correspondence."

Della Street smiled, left the office, and a few moments later was back, carrying a woman's black handbag.

"What's this?" Mason asked.

"This," she said, "is *something*."

"Shoot," Mason said.

"I went to the mail file back in the stenographic office, and in coming back through the reception room noticed this bag in back of the big chair by the door. I asked Gertie if it was hers and she said no, she hadn't seen it before. I asked her who had been in the office carrying a handbag and after a few moments she decided it must have been this mysterious woman who called during the noon hour. The bag was right by the chair she had been occupying."

Mason extended his hand and Della Street gave him the purse.

"Well," Mason said thoughtfully, "that's rather odd. She said she was going out for a few minutes, that she felt she was in some danger, then she didn't come back and it turns out she left her handbag. Of course, we don't know it's hers."

"Think we should look in it?" Della Street asked. "It's heavy enough, it could be full of gold coin."

Mason regarded the exterior of the bag thoughtfully, then said, "I think I'll open it and see if there's a name and address, Della."

The lawyer opened the bag, started to reach in, then jerked his hand back.

"What is it?" Della Street asked.

Mason hesitated a moment, then taking a handkerchief from his pocket wrapped it over his fingers, reached in the handbag and pulled out a blued steel .38-caliber revolver.

"Well, what do you know!" Della Street exclaimed.

Mason, still holding the handkerchief so that he would leave no fingerprints, swung the cylinder out and said, "Four loaded shells, two empty cartridge cases. Thirty-eight caliber. Smith & Wesson revolver."

Mason sniffed the end of the barrel and said, "And apparently it has been discharged rather recently."

Being careful to swing the cylinder back so that the cylinder was in exactly the same position it had been, Mason placed the weapon on the blotter of his desk and said, "Now I guess we'll take an inventory, Della."

Mason regarded the interior of the bag speculatively, then said, "I see a card case in here, Della. Let's take a look at that."

Mason took out the card case, opened it and brought out an assortment of cards.

"Nevada driving license," Mason said. "Adelle Sterling Hastings. 721 Northwest Firston Avenue, Las Vegas, Nevada. . . . Now then, here's a credit card. Mrs. Garvin S. Hastings, 692 Weatherby Boulevard, Los Angeles. And here's a California driving license to Adelle Sterling Hastings, 692 Weatherby Boulevard, Los Angeles.

"Here are quite a few other cards. Membership in the Automobile Club of Southern California as Mrs. Garvin S. Hastings; membership card in a yacht club at Balboa Beach, and three or four credit cards.

"There's a coin purse in here," Mason said, "which seems to be pretty well filled."

Della Street looked up from her notes. "Do you think it's all right to go through *everything* in the handbag?"

Mason said, "It looks very much as if the gun might have been used in a crime, and by leaving the handbag here in the office an attempt is being made to drag me into a case which I may not want to have anything to do with.

"It's not natural for a woman to walk away and leave her purse in someone's office. Unless something has happened to our noonday visitor, I'm beginning to think her leaving the handbag here in the office was a very carefully planned maneuver. If so, I want to find out a lot more about the person who left it."

Mason picked up the coin purse, opened it and said, "Well, *what* do you know?"

Della looked up from her notes.

"Hundred-dollar bills," Mason said. "Fifty-dollar bills. Here's one thousand—fifteen hundred—two thousand—three thousand dollars in big bills, and let's see, twenty—forty—sixty—eighty—ninety—a hundred—a hundred and five—a hundred and ten—a hundred and fifteen dollars in smaller denominations, and some silver amounting to . . . two dollars and forty-three cents.

"Well, Della, our visitor seems to have been financially able to pay a retainer fee."

"Why the past tense?" Della asked.

"Because I don't know whether we're ever going to see her again. You have to admit that any woman who would walk away from a purse with this much money in it and forget all about it must have a very, very short memory. She might even forget what she had used a gun for.

"Now let's see, here's a compact, lipstick, a half-empty pack of cigarettes—here's a key container— Now, that's a peculiar thing, Della. This key container at one time had quite a collection of keys in it. Now there's only one left. You can see where the keys which had been carried in it have left marks on the leather. Now it's down to just one key. . . . However, here's another key container that has half a dozen keys in it, and—"

The telephone rang.

Della answered it, said, "Just a moment, who's calling, please?"

She listened a moment, then placed her hand over the transmitter, turned to Mason and said, "A Mr. Huntley L. Banner, an attorney, says he wants to talk with you about the Hastings' case."

Mason's eyes went from the purse to the gun on the desk. For a moment he hesitated, then nodded, picked up his phone and said, "Yes, Mr. Banner. This is Mason speaking."

The man's voice said, "I'm attorney for Garvin S. Hastings, and I understand you're representing his wife in connection with the property settlement."

"May I ask what gave you that impression?" Mason asked.

"Aren't you?" Banner asked.

Mason laughed and said, "In legal parlance, Mr. Banner, I'm afraid you're avoiding the question. Before I can answer your question I'd like to know just what basis you have for stating that I am representing Mrs. Hastings."

"Well, she told me that you would be representing her."

"May I ask when?"

"Shortly before noon."

"You were talking with her?"

"She talked with my secretary on the telephone."

Mason said cautiously, "I was out of my office when Mrs. Hastings called to see me. She didn't wait. At the moment I don't have any authority to represent her."

"Well," Banner said, "she'll be in to see you again. There's no question that you're her choice for an attorney. You might bear in mind that as far as a settlement is concerned she doesn't have a leg to stand on. All of Hastings' property is separate property. As far as the divorce is concerned, my client has been most co-operative—as far as one can go in such matters without collusion. I think you'll understand what I mean.

"Of course, Hastings doesn't want to see her left without a penny, but I think perhaps she has some exalted ideas in regard to a property settlement. It might be a good thing if she understood right at the start that she isn't going to feather her nest at the expense of my client."

"Isn't there *any* community property?" Mason asked.

"Not worth mentioning. Of course we'll make some sort of a settlement. In fact we'll make a generous settlement."

"Would you care to outline your proposition?" Mason asked.

"Not over the telephone," Banner said.

"Where's your office?" Mason asked.

"In the Grayfrier Building."

"Why, that's only a block and a half away," Mason said. "Look here, Banner, do you have a minute? If you do, I'll come over. There are a couple of things I'd like to find out about the case before I agree to represent Mrs. Hastings."

"If you can come over right away I'll be glad to see you," Banner said.

"Give me five minutes and I'll be there," Mason told him.

Mason hung up the telephone and said to Della, "I'm going over to Banner's office and see if I can get a little of the background on this case. If I start trying to pump him over the telephone he'll get suspicious, but if I go over and visit with him for a while he's apt to do more talking than he really intended to."

Mason left the office and walked down the street to the corner, waited for the signal, crossed the street, walked half a block and entered the Grayfrier Building. He consulted the directory and learned that Banner's entrance office was in Room 438.

The building was a modern steel and concrete structure with a bank of smooth-running elevators, and within a matter of seconds Mason opened the door marked HUNTLEY L. BANNER—*Enter.*

The young woman who sat at a desk facing the door, combining the duties of secretary, stenographer, receptionist and telephone operator, smiled rather vaguely at Mason.

"I'm Perry Mason," he said. "I was talking with Mr. Banner on the telephone and—"

"Oh, yes," she interrupted, coming to life with startling alacrity. "Oh, yes, Mr. Mason!"

She pushed back the secretarial chair, came around the desk, smiled over her shoulder and said, "This way, please."

Mason noted the trim figure, the lithe walk, as she went to the door and opened it.

"Mr. Mason," she announced.

The man who was seated behind the big desk got up and came forward with outstretched hand, his face twisting into a slow smile. He was in his late thirties, chunky in build and had shrewd eyes.

"This is an honor, Counselor," he said. "I'd have been glad to come over and see you but you talked so fast I didn't have a chance to get my thoughts organized.

"This is Miss Mitchell, my secretary, Mr. Mason. She's quite a fan of yours."

The secretary regarded Mason with dark eyes in which there was quite plainly a hint of personalized interest. She extended her hand and said, "I'm delighted to meet you."

Mason took her hand and bowed gravely. "A pleasure, Miss Mitchell."

"See that we're not disturbed," Banner said. "Shut off all telephone calls."

"Oh, it isn't *that* important," Mason said, smiling.

"It is to me," Banner told him. "Sit down, Mr. Mason. Make yourself comfortable. . . . This Hastings case may be rather long and drawn-out, but if your client wants to act sensibly there's no reason why the property settlement part of it can't be handled almost overnight."

"You said you had a proposition in mind that you couldn't outline over the telephone?" Mason suggested.

"Well, I have and I haven't," Banner told him. "Of course, you know the gambit, Mason. I'm not going to be dumb enough to stick my neck out and say, '*Here's what my client will do.*' That would crucify us at some later date.

"So I'll play it the way a smart lawyer should and say, '*This is what I am prepared to advise my client to do.*' That's not binding on my client, it's not binding on me, it's not binding on anyone.

"If you accept the offer and we make a settlement, that's fine. If you don't like the offer, you can't use it against my client and you can't use it against me."

"Fair enough," Mason said. "What's the offer?"

"I will advise my client to pay Adelle Hastings ten thousand dollars a year for a period of five years, or until she remarries, whichever comes first. I will advise him to leave her a flat sum of fifty thousand dollars in his will and provide in the agreement that this bequest is irrevocable unless she predeceases him."

"That's rather an awkward way of handling it," Mason said. "I don't like this idea of a will. How about having him take out a paid-up fifty-thousand-dollar life insurance policy?"

"That *might* be arranged," Banner said. "I have discussed a settlement along these other lines with my client and— Well, you know, Mason, I'm not sticking my neck out, but I'll put it this way: There would be no serious objection on the part of my client to the settlement I have outlined."

"All right," Mason said, "that's your offer. How much—"

"Not an offer, not an offer," Banner said hastily. "It's what I am willing to advise my client to do."

"All right," Mason said, "that's what you are willing to advise your client to do. Now, how much higher will your client go?"

"No higher," Banner said. "That's absolutely tops. We don't do horse-trading around this office, Mason."

"I take it then I either accept that or reject it—in the event I become counsel for Mrs. Hastings."

"Well," Banner said thoughtfully, "we wouldn't want to slam any doors in each other's faces, of course, but that's as high as I'm prepared to advise my client to go. . . . You haven't talked with Mrs. Hastings yet?"

"Not yet," Mason said.

"She's a very charming young woman," Banner said. "She makes a wonderful impression."

"And wears well?" Mason asked.

"And wears well. She's just all right, that girl. I'm terribly sorry her marriage didn't click."

"How long has it been in existence?"

"Around eighteen months."

"Why did it break up?" Mason asked.

Banner shrugged his shoulders. "Why does a man get bald? Why does his hair turn gray?"

"Is it mutual or one-sided?" Mason asked.

"Now look," Banner said, "I don't want to be quoted on this, but Hastings had been married twice before. His first marriage was ideal. His wife died. He became lonely. He looked back on that first marriage and forgot all the bickering, all the little, everyday nagging things that happen in a marriage and remembered only the rosy glow.

"So Hastings married again. He didn't realize his first happiness hinged upon the personality of his wife. He began to think that because he had been so happy before it must have been the state of matrimony rather than the personality of the woman. So he tried this second marriage. That marriage just didn't work. It ended in a divorce. Then after a while Hastings got lonely again and married Adelle. That was his third marriage. Adelle was his secretary. She was sympathetic, kind and considerate.

"The only reason Hastings wasn't happy was because he wasn't happy. I don't think he knows the reason and I'm sure I don't."

"So Adelle Hastings said she was consulting me?" Mason asked.

"That's right. She telephoned the office. I was out. She talked with my secretary, said she had driven in from Las Vegas and was going to put her affairs in your hands."

"I'm rather an unusual choice for a lawyer in a divorce settlement," Mason said. "Mostly my practice concerns crimes of violence and things of that sort."

"I know, I know, but nevertheless you're a glamorous figure and any lawyer who can make a spectacular success out of murder cases can handle divorce settlements with one hand tied behind him.

"I'm going to be perfectly fair with you, Mason. When Elvina told me that you were going to be representing Adelle I gave a little inward shudder."

"Elvina?" Mason asked.

"Elvina Mitchell, my secretary."

"I see," Mason said. "Well, I guess I'll be in touch with you a little later on then. . . . Care to comment on the amount of property involved?"

"There isn't any," Banner said.

"What!" Mason exclaimed. "I thought you were talking about ten thousand dollars a year and—"

"I was. I am," Banner said. "You asked about the amount of property *involved* and I tell you there isn't any. There's lots of property but it isn't involved in the case and it isn't going to be involved in the case. It's all my client's separate property. Hastings can do what he likes with it. If he wants to make a settlement with Adelle so that she can get along for a while without having to go back to work, he can do so. If he doesn't want to give her anything, I don't know of anything anyone can do about it."

"Then what was the reason you became concerned when you thought Adelle was going to consult with me?"

Banner laughed. "It's just the idea of going up against a champ."

"Well," Mason said, grinning, "I'll be on my way. I just wanted to get acquainted with you and get a fill-in on the background. I take it Adelle is applying for divorce or is going to apply for divorce."

"She's established a residence in Las Vegas. She's filing for divorce the first of next week. Now of course, Mason, you and I both realize that we can't have any collusion or that would destroy the validity of the divorce, but within reasonable limits we want to co-operate in every way we can so as to expedite matters.

"For instance, you can have a summons issued and arrange for service but I'll appear on behalf of Garvin Hastings and file an answer, a sort of general denial. Then the case will be set down for trial and I won't show up—provided, of course, we've reached a property settlement in the meantime.

"That will enable you to short-cut all the delay incident to publication of summons and it will give a valid action because the court will have jurisdiction over both parties and we can have jurisdiction of personam as well as an action in rem."

"Why this desire to expedite things?" Mason asked. "Has Hastings some other woman in mind?"

Banner smiled and shook his head. "I can state now without fear of contradiction that Hastings has been cured. I think that's the reason the marriage fell apart. Hastings is just a rugged individual who likes to live his own life in his own way. He's completely absorbed in his business and I don't think the guy really cares about a home life except on occasion when he gets a little lonely living in a big house all by himself.

"And you can tell your client this, Mason, that any time she wants to go back to work for the Hastings Enterprises as a secretary she can do it. Hastings is very fond of her—as a secretary. There isn't going to be any mud-slinging, any name-calling or any friction. This whole matter is going to be handled amicably and on a friendly basis. Hastings is really going all out to see that his wife gets a decent settlement."

"Thanks a lot," Mason said, shaking hands. "I'll doubtless be seeing you."

As Mason left the office Elvina Mitchell flashed him a warm smile. "Good-by, Mr. Mason," she said.

"Bye now," Mason said. "I'll be seeing you."

Mason returned to his office, grinned at Della Street and said, "Guess I'm getting to be a little jumpy. It's all right, Della. Just a divorce property settlement with some interesting background."

"What about the gun and the two shells that have been fired?" Della asked.

"That," Mason said, "is something else. But there's certainly no reason for her to fire the two bullets into her husband and apparently she doesn't have any rival, so we'll assume she took a couple of pot shots at a jack rabbit on the way in from Las Vegas.

"Let's get at that pile of mail and see how much of it we can get done before Adelle Hastings comes in."

Mason started dictating but after a while his attention began to wander. He glanced from time to time at his wrist watch and there were long periods of silence.

At four o'clock Della Street said, "If you're going to worry about it, why don't we try telephoning?"

"Do that," Mason said. "Telephone Las Vegas. See if there's a telephone in the name of Adelle Hastings at the address given on that driving license."

Della Street put through the call, then after a few moments said, "There's a phone listed. They're ringing and get no answer."

Mason said, "Ring the residence of Garvin Hastings. Don't give any name. Just ask if you can talk to Mrs. Hastings. It may be she went out there to negotiate a settlement on her own. In fact the more I think of it the more I feel that's the explanation. She came in here to see me, then decided to call her husband to tell him what she was doing, and he suggested she come out and talk with him." Mason snapped his fingers. "Why didn't I think of that before? That's the only really logical explanation."

Della Street nodded, looked up the number of the Garvin Hastings residence, put through the call, listened a moment, then gently hung up the telephone.

"What?" Mason asked.

"A tape-recording answering service," she said. "A well-modulated voice on a tape says that Mr. Hastings is not available at the moment, that following the notice on the tape there will be a period of thirty seconds during which the person calling can leave any message. This message will be recorded on tape and brought to the attention of Mr. Hastings on his return."

"Okay," Mason said, "forget it. It's probably all right."

"And what do we do with the purse, the money and the gun?" Della Street asked. "Do we hold them here in the office?"

Mason said, "Between now and five o'clock we'll have a call from Adelle Hastings. She'll suddenly realize where it was she left her bag."

"Want to bet?" Della Street asked.

Mason grinned. "No," he said.

TWO

At five-fifteen Della Street said, "How about it, Chief, do we close up the office? It's five-fifteen."

Mason nodded, said, "I guess there's nothing else to do, Della."

"Are you going to worry about this all night?" she asked.

"I don't know," Mason admitted. "I can't get it out of my mind. I have a hunch we should charter a plane and fly to Las Vegas."

"But she isn't there," Della Street said.

"Her apartment's there," Mason pointed out, "and we probably have a key to it."

"What would be in her apartment?"

"Possibly a clue," Mason said. "Possibly nothing."

"Would you go into her apartment?"

"I don't know," Mason said. "I'll cross that bridge when I come to it, and I *would* like to know what time she gets home."

"You think she's headed back to Las Vegas?"

Mason said, "If she isn't, she's in bad trouble. She left my office. She probably had her car parked. She may have gone to get something out of the car and—"

"How do you deduce all that?" Della Street asked.

"From her purse."

"You mean the things in her purse?"

"The things that are *not* in her purse," Mason said.

Della Street raised inquiring eyebrows.

Mason said, "She was in Las Vegas. She has a Nevada driving license. She drives an automobile. She probably drove in from Las

Vegas. That would mean she drove to my office building. She had to do something with her automobile. There's a parking lot next door. She probably put the car in that parking lot. She was given a parking receipt. She put that in her purse. She came up to my office. She was terribly excited. Regardless of what had caused her excitement, we know that she had probably fired a thirty-eight-caliber revolver at something, firing two shots.

"Then she remembered that there was something in the car that she wanted. She must have taken the receipt out of her purse and gone down to the parking lot.

"When she arrived there something happened to keep her from returning to the office.

"Now then, the question is: Did she leave her purse purposely or accidentally?"

"Why would she leave it purposely?"

"Because," Mason said, "it had that gun in it. She didn't want to be carrying that purse around with her any more than necessary. She intended to come right back. She told Gertie she'd be back within a matter of five minutes.

"If she wanted to get something out of her car, she probably wanted to tip the attendant. She took along probably a fifty-cent piece and the parking receipt, intending to tip the attendant. Then something happened that caused her to change her plans."

Mason was thoughtfully silent, then said, "Della, give Paul Drake a ring. See if he's left his office. If he hasn't, ask him to come down here right away. I've got a job for him."

"How about all this?" Della Street asked, indicating the contents of the purse which had been arranged on Mason's desk.

Mason opened a drawer of his desk. Picking the gun up with his handkerchief, he dropped it into the drawer. The other articles he returned to the purse.

Della rang Paul Drake at the Drake Detective Agency, talked briefly, then hung up and said to Perry Mason, "He was just leaving the office. I caught him at the door. He said he'd be right down."

A moment later Drake's code knock sounded on the exit door of Mason's private office and Della Street opened it.

"That's the worst of having a detective agency on the same floor as your clients," Drake said. "You never get away. . . . Now look,

Perry, I hope this isn't a big job. I've got something I want to do tonight."

Drake moved over to the client's big overstuffed chair, draped himself over the rounded leather arm and grinned at the lawyer.

Mason said, "This is a detective job that I want done fast. I should have had it done two or three hours earlier. I hope I'm not too late."

Paul Drake, tall, loose-jointed, shock-proofed against any surprise, slid back into the chair, his long legs over the rounded arm. He reached for a cigarette. His manner was completely relaxed.

"Shoot," he said.

Mason said, "You're pretty well known down at the parking lot next door, Paul?"

"I should be," Drake said, grinning. "I've kept my car there for seven years."

Mason said, "So have I. That's the reason I can't do this myself. As a detective you have the right to prowl around without people asking too many questions. I'd attract too much attention."

"What do you want me to do?" Drake asked.

Mason said, "Go down to that parking lot, Paul. Cover every automobile that's left in it. Look for Nevada license plates. Whenever you find a car with Nevada license plates, write down the license number and look to see if there's a registration certificate on the steering post of the car. If there is, get the owner's name but get the license numbers of every Nevada automobile that's in that parking lot."

"Right now?" Drake asked.

"Right *now!*" Mason said. "I should have been smart and had it done three hours ago."

Drake gave him a quizzical look, then slid his tall frame to an upright position and without a word walked out of the door.

"Charter service?" Della Street asked.

"We'll wait on Paul Drake," Mason said. "If her car's down there, we'll start looking at this end."

"And if it isn't?"

"We fly to Las Vegas."

"Do we eat first?"

"We eat afterwards," Mason said, "unless you want a hamburger or a hot dog to tide you over."

Della Street moved over to the telephone, called the restaurant and lunch counter which occupied one corner of the parking lot.

"Can you," she asked, "prepare two hamburger sandwiches which we can pick up in about twenty minutes? This is Della Street, Perry Mason's secretary. . . . That's right. Mr. Mason wants his with lots of onion and relish. I like mine with lots of relish and not *quite* so much onion. Start on them right away, please."

Della Street hung up the phone.

Mason looked at his watch, grinned, said, "What about Paul, Della?"

"Paul," Della said, "has something on for tonight. He'll probably dine on filet mignon, baked potato, French-fried onions and a nice salad, all washed down with a bottle of vintage wine.

"And," she continued, "if you give him an opportunity, he'll charge the whole business on the expense account and hand you the bill."

Within fifteen minutes Drake's code knock sounded on the door. Della Street opened it, and Drake, coming in, said, "Only two Nevada licenses in the parking lot, Perry."

"Find out who owns the cars?"

"There are no registration certificates. One of the licenses is ATK 205. I asked a few questions and got the parking lot attendant to tell me how long the car had been there. The car's been parked there six hours.

"The other car has license number SFU 804. It's been there for eight hours."

Mason nodded to Della Street. "All right, Paul, get in touch with the Nevada police. I want a run-down on those license numbers. Then get in touch with your correspondents in the proper cities in Nevada and get a line on the people who own the cars. I want just the general background, nothing too detailed at present. So far I'm doing this on my own, so keep the expenses somewhere within reason."

"What do you mean, within reason?"

"Well," Mason said, "Della was pointing out that you probably were on your way to keep a date, that you'd dine on filet mignon with all the fixings, washed down with a bottle of vintage wine, and the whole thing would be on the expense account."

"Not if I'm going to be sitting on a telephone," Drake said.

"You don't have to," Mason told him. "Ring up the Nevada police. Get the names of the owners of the cars and their addresses. I'll telephone you in about thirty-five or forty minutes. You should be able to have the information by that time. Then get your correspondents working on the case and go out to dinner. By the time they dig out the information and telephone it in, you'll be back in your office."

"And dinner's on the expense account?"

"I reckon."

Drake grinned. "This *is* a break! Usually, when I'm on one of your cases, I wind up having a soggy hamburger for dinner with sodium bicarbonate for dessert. . . . I'm on my way."

Mason nodded to Della Street.

They hurried down to the restaurant where Della picked up the hamburgers, which they ate on their way to the airport.

THREE

From the airport Mason telephoned Paul Drake. "Got the dope on those Nevada cars yet, Paul?"

"Just got it," Drake said. "Car with license number ATK 205 is registered to Melina Finch, 625 Cypress Avenue, Las Vegas. License number SFU 804 is registered to Harley C. Drexel, 291 Center Street, Carson City. Got that?"

"Give it to me once more," Mason said. "I want to check and make sure I have it right."

Drake repeated the names and addresses, together with the license numbers.

Mason snapped his notebook shut, said, "I've got it. Now then, Paul, get your correspondents to check on these people."

"I don't have any correspondent in Carson City," Drake said. "Reno is the nearest place. That's thirty miles away and it'll take a little while for my correspondents to get a man on the job."

"Try and have it by midnight, if you can," Mason said.

He hung up the phone.

Della Street said, "The pilot's all ready."

Mason and Della Street hurried over to the twin-engine charter plane.

Mason said to the pilot, "We want to go to Las Vegas. You can wait for us there. We'll be coming back tonight. Everything okay?"

"Roger," the pilot said.

They fastened their seat belts, the motors revved up, and the pilot, getting clearance from the tower, swept down the runway into the air and after climbing to elevation set a course for Las Vegas.

The sun, low in the west, illuminated the mountains as they flew high over the cities in the valley. They encountered turbulence over the mountains and leaving the timbered peaks behind, flew high over the purple shadows of the desert.

It was dark by the time they landed in Las Vegas.

"You wait," Mason said. "I'm sorry I can't give you any definite time of departure. It'll be more than an hour and it may be longer, but have it all gassed up and ready to go."

"Will do," the pilot said. "I'd like to start before midnight, if possible."

"Flying difficulties?" Mason asked.

"Marital difficulties," the pilot said. "My wife takes a dim view of these trips to Las Vegas—if I don't get back before morning."

"Get many such trips?" Mason asked.

"Well, it depends," the pilot said, grinning. "From my viewpoint, I don't get enough. From the wife's viewpoint I get a lot too many."

"We'll let you know," Mason said, "as soon as we know. But I feel certain we'll be underway before midnight."

A taxicab took them to 721 Northwest Firston Avenue.

As Mason had surmised, it was an apartment house.

He looked at the directory, found the name Adelle S. Hastings, and rang the bell.

There was no answer.

"Now what?" Della Street asked.

Mason said, "Under the circumstances I think we're justified in just *trying* the keys."

Della Street said uneasily, "I feel that we should have some sort of an official status here. How about calling the police—just asking them to stand by?"

Mason shook his head. "Not yet, Della. Our client— Well, when you come right down to it, she isn't a client but we *are* protecting her to the best of our ability anyway."

"Protecting her from what?" Della Street asked.

"That," Mason said, "is one of the things we're trying to find out. We may be protecting her from herself."

"But you don't think so?"

"I don't know."

Mason opened his brief case, took out the two key containers, started fitting keys to the outer door of the apartment house.

Key after key proved unavailing.

"Looks like we've drawn a blank," Della Street said.

"We have one last one," Mason said.

He inserted the key and the lock clicked back.

"Well," Mason said, "this seems to be it."

Della Street hesitated as Mason held the door of the apartment house open for her.

"Go on," the lawyer told her, "it's Apartment 289."

"But why go up?" Della Street said. "We know now that the key fits. We know it's her purse. We know she isn't home and—"

"How do we know she isn't home?" Mason asked.

"Because she doesn't answer the doorbell."

Mason said, "She might not care to have visitors or she might not be able to answer the doorbell."

Della Street thought that over for a moment, then marched through the open door and down the corridor to the elevator.

They took the elevator to the second floor, found Apartment 289, and Mason pressed the mother-of-pearl button by the side of the door. They heard chimes on the inside but there was no sound of answering motion from within the apartment.

Mason tapped on the door with his knuckles.

After a moment the lawyer said, "Della, I know how irregular this is, but I'm going in. Perhaps you'd better wait here."

"Why?" she asked.

"I'm just going to make sure that there isn't a body in there."

"You mean hers?"

"I don't know," Mason said. "Those two bullets that had been fired from that revolver must have hit *something*."

The lawyer, using the same key which had fit the lock on the outside door, clicked back the latch lock and opened the door. He groped for and found the light switch. He turned on the lights.

It was apparently a three-room apartment with the living room in front, a door on the side evidently opening into a bedroom, while another door—which was standing open—disclosed a small kitchen. Apparently the apartment had been rented furnished but was considerably above the average run of furnished apartments rented to persons who came to Nevada to take up a brief residence, secure a divorce and then leave.

"Well," Mason said, "so far no bodies—and very little indicating the personality of the occupant.

"There are a few books over there and the usual run of magazines on the table—an ash tray with two cigarette stubs in it and one glass with— The devil!"

"What?" Della Street exclaimed, at the tone of Mason's voice.

Mason pointed to the glass. "Ice cubes," he said.

"Good heavens! Then somebody has been here and—"

The door from the bedroom opened. A woman wearing a bathing cap with a robe draped around her stood looking at them with indignant eyes.

"Go right ahead," she said. "Make yourself right at home! Don't mind me."

"I'm terribly sorry," Mason said, "but I had no idea you were home. I knocked and rang the bell. I telephoned you earlier in the day and had no answer."

"I've been in Los Angeles all day," she said. "Now will you kindly tell me who you are, how you got in and what you want, or shall I call the police?"

Mason said, "I'm Perry Mason, an attorney in Los Angeles. Why didn't you return to my office?"

"*Return* to your office?" she asked.

"Yes."

She said, "I've never been in your office in my life and I have an idea that you're not a lawyer at all. Who's that with you?"

"Miss Della Street, my secretary," Mason said.

"How did you get in?"

"We used your key," Mason said.

"What do you mean, *my* key?"

"Exactly what I said. You left your key in my office—together with some other things."

She said, "If you don't get out of here I'm going to—"

Abruptly she turned and raced into the bedroom, leaving the bedroom door open.

Mason saw her whip open a drawer in a bedstand, then plunge her hand inside, grope around for a moment, then turn back to the door with an expression of amazement on her face.

She whirled and picked up a telephone by the side of the bed.

"I think I'd better get the police after all," she said.

"Wait a minute," Mason told her, "are you *quite* sure you want the police?"

"Why not?"

Mason said, "You left your handbag in my office you know. There were quite a few things in it."

"*My* handbag in *your* office?"

"Yes. Didn't you miss it?"

Slowly she lowered her hand and dropped the telephone back into its cradle.

"Now," she said, "I think you had better start talking."

Mason said, "I think *you'd* better take the initiative, Mrs. Hastings. I can assure you that I'm here because I was trying to help you. I was very much concerned about you when you didn't return to my office and I found that you had left your handbag, your purse, driving licenses, keys and . . . that other thing."

"What other thing?"

Mason indicated the bedstand with its open drawer. "The thing you pretended to be looking for just now, and I would like to compliment you on your acting ability. I certainly hope you can do as well when you get in front of a jury."

She regarded him thoughtfully for a moment, then said, "Mr. Mason—if you really are Perry Mason—do you have my handbag?"

Mason nodded.

"How did you get it?"

"You came to my office a little after noon today and left it there when you went out."

"I wasn't in your office at all. I have heard the name Perry Mason. I lived in Los Angeles with my husband for some time and have seen your name mentioned in the papers from time to time. I have never been in your office in my life."

"Your bag?" Mason asked.

"My bag was stolen from my automobile sometime yesterday. I was in Los Angeles. I wanted cigarettes. I found a parking place in front of a store, grabbed a dollar bill from my change purse, dashed into the store, picked up a package of cigarettes and— Well, when I came out my purse was gone—although I didn't miss it until later."

"I see," Mason said, smiling slightly. "Now, if you had the presence of mind to complain to the police that your purse had been stolen, you just *might* have a story the jury would believe."

"Why should there be a jury? Why shouldn't they believe my story? What possible object would I have in making up such a story?"

"I take it then you didn't complain to the police."

"As a matter of fact I didn't, although I don't see where it concerns you in the least."

"Why didn't you complain to the police?"

"Because," she said, "for one thing, I didn't know it was gone until I arrived at my home in Los Angeles and looked for my key and found the whole bag was gone.

"You see, I was on my way to keep an appointment with my husband. I was afraid I was going to be late and he is a stickler for promptness, so I was in a hurry. For that reason I didn't put the cigarettes in my bag but just tossed them on the seat. The bag must have been gone at that time. In fact, that was the only time it could have been taken, but I didn't notice it until I got to my house and reached for my key container."

"Why didn't you notify the police then?" Mason asked.

"My husband said it would be a waste of time and— Well, he didn't want it known that I was spending the night there in our house. You see, we've separated and—"

"Was your reluctance to call the police due in part to the fact that there was something else in your bag?" Mason asked. "The something that you were looking for just now in the drawer by the side of the bed?"

"The gun?" she asked.

"Yes."

"My gun wasn't in the handbag," she said. "For all I knew it was in that drawer in the stand by the bed. Someone evidently has taken the gun, presumably the same person who stole my handbag, since the keys to this apartment were in the handbag—and now *you* show up with those keys. Perhaps it is *your* story that should be checked, Mr. Mason."

"You didn't take the gun with you on your trip to Los Angeles?"

"Certainly not. I went in to Los Angeles to keep my appointment. I drove back this afternoon and got in just about twenty minutes ago. I smoked a couple of cigarettes, had a drink, and was taking a shower when I heard voices out here. . . . Now then, Mr. Mason, if you have my bag I'll trouble you to return it."

Mason said, "I'd like to ask a couple of questions first."

"You have no right to ask questions—no more right to have your questions answered than you had to take my key and make an illegal entry into this apartment."

Abruptly Mason became crisply businesslike. "You went in to Los Angeles yesterday?"

"Yes."

"You had an appointment with your husband?"

"Yes, I tell you."

"You kept it?"

"Yes."

"What did you want to see your husband about?"

"That's none of your business."

"A property settlement?"

"I say it's none of your business."

"You didn't reach any agreement with him?"

"Again, that's none of your business, Mr. Mason."

"Where did you spend the night last night?"

"For your information, I spent it in my own home, but there again, that's none of your business."

Mason said, "Look here, Mrs. Hastings, if you're lying, and apparently you are, you've worked out what you feel is a very ingenious lie. But I warn you that you can't get away with it. The police are too thorough and too clever."

"I'll worry about my affairs, Mr. Mason. You worry about yours."

Mason said, "The bag which you left in my office shortly after noon had your driving license, a purse with a considerable sum of money in it, keys, and a gun; and for your information, two of the cartridges in that gun had been freshly discharged."

"What!" she exclaimed, her eyes growing large.

Mason said, "You're a very convincing actress. There are times when I find myself believing your story, and I believe it very much against my better judgment."

Adelle Hastings moved over to a chair, abruptly sat down as though her knees refused to support her weight.

"Won't you . . . won't you sit down?" she asked.

Mason nodded to Della Street.

They took chairs.

She said at length, "Mr. Mason, you've entered my apartment unlawfully for a purpose I don't quite understand. Lawyerlike, you've managed to put me on the defensive by asking me questions and talking about my story not being true. Now I'd like to find out about *your* story."

Mason said, "My story can be vouched for by my secretary and by my office receptionist. She said you arrived about twelve-twenty, shortly after Miss Street and I had gone out for lunch. She said that you told her that you had to leave the office for just a moment, that you would be right back, but you never returned.

"Then, later on in the afternoon, we found this handbag by the chair where you had been sitting. Naturally we didn't know it was yours at the time. I took it into my private office and Miss Street and I made an inventory of the contents."

"Did you," she asked, "open the coin purse?"

"Yes."

"What did you find in there?"

"Money."

"How much money?"

Mason nodded his head to Della Street.

Della Street took a notebook from her purse, said, "Three thousand, one hundred and seventeen dollars and forty-three cents."

"And a gun was in there?"

"Yes."

"You say it had been fired twice?"

"Yes."

"Where . . . where is that gun now?"

"In a drawer in my office."

"Where is my bag with the contents?"

"I have it with me."

"Have you," she asked, "some way of proving that you're Perry Mason?"

"Certainly," Mason said.

He took a folder from his pocket, showed her his driving license and credit cards.

"Well," she said at length, "I guess I have to accept your story. Where's my handbag?"

"In my brief case here," Mason said.

"Well, at least I can have that back."

"You can when you have convinced me that you're Adelle Hastings or Mrs. Garvin S. Hastings."

"But I can't convince you. You have all the proof—it's in the handbag and you have that."

Mason said, "And I'm not going to turn that handbag over to anyone until I'm positive of the identification."

She thought for a moment, said, "If you have my bag, you have a folder containing my driving licenses."

Mason nodded.

"The California driving license," she said, "has a thumbprint on it and also my picture."

"The picture," Mason said, "isn't good enough to suit me."

"There's the thumbprint," she said. "That should convince you."

She walked over to a writing desk, opened it, spilled a little ink from a bottle onto a blotter, pressed her thumb against the blotter, then pressed it against a sheet of writing paper several times.

"I think these impressions are clear enough," she said. "You should be able to make a comparison from those."

"You don't happen to have a magnifying glass, do you?" Mason asked.

"No, I don't. I— Wait a minute, I do, too. Just a moment."

She opened another drawer in the writing desk and rummaged around among some odds and ends and then produced a magnifying glass.

Mason opened his brief case, reached in, took out the card case, turned to the thumbprint on the California driving license and carefully compared the thumbprint with the thumbprints on the paper she had given him.

Satisfied, at length, the lawyer took the handbag from the brief case and said, "It's all here except the gun. I'm holding that."

"Why?"

"It may be evidence."

"Of what?"

"Murder."

She looked at him wordlessly, panic in her eyes.

"Where did you get the gun?" Mason asked.

"My husband gave it to me."

"Where did he get it?"

"He bought it."

"Why did he give it to you?"

"For my protection, because I do a little driving at night."

"What happened last night?"

"My husband and I reached an agreement."

"On a property settlement?"

"Yes."

"Know an attorney by the name of Banner?" Mason asked.

"Huntley L. Banner?" she asked, her voice dripping with distaste."

"Yes. Who is he?"

"He's my husband's attorney, and I think it is largely due to him that my marriage split up."

"It split up?"

She made an inclusive, sweeping gesture with her hand, indicating the apartment. "What do you think I'm doing here?" she said. "I'm establishing a residence."

"So you can get a divorce?"

"Yes."

"It's amicable?"

"Of course. My husband is paying all my expenses."

"I had a talk with Banner this afternoon," Mason said.

"*You* did?"

"That's right."

"How did you happen to get in touch with him?"

"I didn't," Mason said. "He got in touch with me. He said that you had telephoned his office that you were going to put your affairs in my hands for the purpose of negotiating a property settlement."

"Why in the world would he say a thing like that? I never called him and there was no need for me to get a lawyer. My husband and I reached an agreement without any difficulty. We had been holding off to see what developed in connection with certain oil property."

"Banner said he had been authorized to make a deal on a property settlement," Mason said.

She said, "I just can't understand it."

"Understand what?" Mason asked.

"The fact that Garvin didn't call Huntley Banner and tell him that everything had been fixed up. . . . What time was it he called you?"

"Around two o'clock or so this afternoon, perhaps a little after two. I didn't make a note of the time."

"Why, Garvin was going to call him first thing in the morning."

"That was this morning?"

"Yes."

"Evidently," Mason said, "he didn't do it. Is there any reason why he wouldn't have done it?"

"No. He told me he was going to and I knew he would keep his word."

"Evidently," Mason said, "he *didn't* keep his word."

"I just can't understand that. It's not like him. He—"

Mason indicated the telephone. "Suppose you call him right now," he said, "and ask him what the score is."

"That's a good idea," she said.

She went to the telephone, called long distance and said, "I want to put through a collect call to Garvin S. Hastings in Los Angeles. That's a person-to-person call and I want the charges reversed. This is Mrs. Hastings calling."

She gave the operator her number and the number of the Los Angeles telephone and settled down to wait.

"Do you always call him collect?" Mason asked.

"Yes," she said. "He likes it that way. It gives him an opportunity to know I'm calling and where I'm calling from. He doesn't like to have someone just call him on the telephone and not know who it is."

"Doesn't he have a secretary to handle the telephone?" Mason asked.

"Not at the house at night. He . . ."

She broke off and said into the telephone, "Are you sure? . . . No, I guess that's all right. Just cancel, please."

She dropped the telephone into place, looked up at Mason and said, "I can't understand it. The long distance operator says a tape recording connection is on. That's an answering service Garvin has when you call and a voice answers stating it's a tape recording, that you will have thirty seconds after the voice ceases talking to transmit any message you may wish, that the message will be recorded on the tape so it can be played back when the subscriber returns to answer the telephone personally."

"I tried calling that number," Mason said, "and got the same message."

"You did?"

"Yes."

"When?"

"This afternoon after we had inventoried the contents of your purse."

"But I can't understand it," she said. "I just can't understand why Garvin didn't call up Huntley Banner and tell him."

"He was to do that this morning?"

"Yes."

"You weren't there this morning?"

"No," she said. "I had other appointments."

Mason said, "You just arrived here a short time ago. It didn't take you all day to drive from Los Angeles here."

"I had something else to do."

"What?"

"I don't think I care to tell you any more, Mr. Mason."

"All right," Mason said. "We'll start putting two and two together. You were with your husband last night."

"Yes."

"You reached a property settlement with him."

"Yes."

"He was to telephone his lawyer, Huntley Banner, and tell him to draw up the necessary papers for you to sign. He was to do that early this morning."

"Yes."

"Banner hasn't heard from your husband," Mason said. "Your handbag was stolen yesterday. It was left in my office around noon today. There was a thirty-eight-caliber revolver in that handbag. A woman, wearing large dark glasses which would make it exceedingly difficult to recognize her, came to my office shortly after noon, told the receptionist her name was Hastings, that she had to see me upon a matter of the greatest importance, that she was in danger, that she needed protection and a private detective.

"Then after a few minutes she said she had to leave the office, that she'd be right back. She left and didn't come back. She left your handbag in my office. In that handbag was your gun. It had been fired twice.

"Your husband didn't do the things he was supposed to have done today. He isn't answering the telephone.

"Now then, Mrs. Hastings, just suppose that some woman had stolen your handbag, had gone to your husband's house shortly after you left this morning, had fired two shots and your husband is lying there very, very dead. Where do you suppose that's going to leave you?"

Her face blanched, then suddenly her eyes became suspicious. "Now, just minute," she said. And then after a moment added, "So *that's* your game."

"What is?"

"You're representing some client who stole my handbag and now you're going to try to make me the goat."

"My mysterious client stole your handbag before you saw your husband?" Mason asked.

"Yes. That's when it was stolen."

"You told your husband about your handbag having been stolen?"

"Yes, of course."

"You were alone with him last night?"

"Yes."

"You had no money?"

"I had no money when I arrived," she said. "My husband gave me five hundred dollars as get-by money. I bought a new handbag and coin purse."

"And operated your automobile without a driving license?"

"Yes."

"You didn't make an affidavit your license had been lost?"

"No. I was going to do that this evening. I was going to report to the police that my handbag had been stolen."

"Were you going to tell them about the gun being listed in the contents?"

"Certainly not. I had no idea the gun was in the handbag."

Mason said, "I came here in a chartered plane. I'm going to fly back to Los Angeles. I wanted to get this thing straightened out. I was afraid you might be in danger. I suggest that you come back with me, that you go to your house and investigate for yourself. . . . Does your husband have a secretary who comes in during the day?"

"Not unless he sends for one. He has his office and goes up there for most of his work."

"Did he have any appointments for today?"

"I don't know."

"You wouldn't be able to find out whether he had kept his appointments?"

She said, "I might call Simley Beason."

"Who's he?"

"The office manager and general business manager. He's very close to Garvin, my husband."

"Closer than Banner?"

"Oh, Banner," she said, spitting the name out with disgust, "is just a lawyer who tries to keep pushing his way in on things. I wish Garvin could see him in his true light, but he has Garvin completely hypnotized. Believe you me, Banner doesn't have Simley Beason hypnotized. Simley knows exactly the sort of man Banner is—an opportunist, a selfish, scheming, conniving lawyer who keeps trying to get my husband to rely on him more and more in matters of business as well as in matters of law. . . . I'm going to call Simley."

She picked up the telephone and placed a person-to-person long distance call to Simley Beason.

"You have his house number?" Mason asked.

"Yes, of course. . . . Oh, don't be so damned suspicious, Mr. Mason. That's the trouble with you lawyers. . . . I did some of my husband's secretarial work after I was married. I was his secretary before we were married. I've called Simley Beason a hundred times at—

"Hello, hello, Simley? This is Adelle Hastings. . . . I'm fine. . . . Yes, in Las Vegas. . . . That's right, I drove to Los Angeles yesterday. I came back just a short while ago. . . . Well, that's fine. . . . Simley, tell me, I'm trying to get hold of Garvin and he doesn't answer. The answering service is on and— What? . . . He didn't say anything? . . . Well, that's strange. . . . No, no, I guess it's all right. Probably something happened that caused him to leave town . . . but that's not like him. . . . Well, thanks a lot. I'm sorry I bothered you. I wanted to get in touch with him. I'll call him again tomorrow. Look, Simley, let me know if you hear anything, will you? Tell him I want to see him.

"Well, it's not exactly confidential; that is, in a way it is and in a way it isn't. I reached an agreement with him on property matters and . . . well, thanks a lot. I knew you'd be pleased. . . . I don't know. He was to call Huntley Banner first thing this morning. Apparently he didn't do so. Banner still thinks he's in the saddle and is still trying to negotiate a property settlement, as he calls it. Actually what he's trying to do is to make himself indispensable so that Garvin will put more and more reliance on him. . . . I know you do, Simley. . . . You know that I'm not greedy. I know it isn't community property, but I *did* give up a good job, a career and my business connections and I was a good wife to Garvin for at least eighteen months. . . . Frankly, I think things would have been all right if it hadn't been for that Banner person. . . . Well, I know you've got other things to do than sit and talk about Huntley Banner over the telephone. Tell Garvin when you see him that I've been trying to get in touch with him, will you? . . . He'll be sure to be in tomorrow morning if he has that appointment. . . . All right, thanks. Bye now."

She hung up the phone and said to Mason, "My husband wasn't in his office all day, which is strange, although he didn't have any appointments; but he did have some important correspondence he wanted to dictate. However, he has a *very* important appointment tomorrow morning at ten o'clock and he'll be sure to be there for that."

"Provided he's keeping appointments," Mason said.

She said, "Mr. Mason, you have one of those damnable legal minds. You always think of the worst that can happen. You almost had me convinced that my husband was lying dead, shot with my gun."

"And," Mason said, "I've almost convinced myself of it now."

She said, "You're getting more and more like Huntley Banner— No, now I didn't mean that. That's uncalled for. I meant to say that you lawyers are all alike— No, that isn't what I wanted to say either, but my husband has a lot of irons in the fire. He has a lot of important business affairs and I don't think there's any question that something happened that called him out of town unexpectedly and since he didn't have any important appointments at the office he just didn't show up."

"And didn't telephone?" Mason asked.

Her eyes narrowed for a moment. She said, "You have a point there. If he doesn't show up by ten o'clock tomorrow morning for that appointment—but he will."

Mason said, "I made one suggestion to you, Mrs. Hastings. I am going back to Los Angeles in a chartered plane. I think you had better fly back with us and see if everything is all right at your house."

"And suppose it isn't all right?" she said.

"Then you can notify the police."

"Yes," she said, "that would really knock the props out from under my story, wouldn't it? I'd go to the police and tell them that I had flown in from Las Vegas because it suddenly occurred to me something had happened to my husband."

"I'd go in with you," Mason said. "We'd go to the house together. If there's anything wrong we'll notify the police and I'll take the responsibility."

"And if there isn't anything wrong," she said, "my husband would just raise merry hell, Mr. Mason, both with you and with me. It probably wouldn't make any difference to you, but as far as I'm concerned it would ruin a perfectly good property settlement.

"Thank you very much for returning my things to me, Mr. Mason, and I think after all I'll let you look over the property settlement after Huntley Banner draws it up, because I don't trust him for a minute."

"And the gun?" Mason asked.

"The gun," she said, and frowned. "You're sure two shells had been fired?"

"Yes."

"I always kept it fully loaded," she said.

"And someone stole it?" Mason asked.

"Certainly. I've told you that."

"You're not going back with us?" Mason asked.

"No, and I wish you'd stop interesting yourself in the case. You've found out that I'm all right now, and you've returned my handbag. I think that I'll be in touch with you again, but I don't want you to . . . well, I don't want you to rock the boat. Do you understand?"

"I understand," Mason said.

FOUR

The pilot of the chartered plane came to meet the taxicab as Mason and Della drove up at the airport.

"Well, this is a surprise," he said. "I didn't expect you people for a couple of hours yet. What happened, did you lose all your money gambling?"

"Every cent of it," Mason said, grinning.

"Don't let him kid you," Della said. "He was thinking about your wife."

"Well, this is really going to surprise her," the pilot said. "You're ready to go back?"

"On our way," Mason said.

They went over to the airplane, climbed in, fastened seat belts, the pilot warmed up the motors and took off to make a wide, sweeping turn over the brilliantly lighted business district of Las Vegas.

Looking down at the lights, Della said, "I'll bet that takes a lot of money out of a lot of different states. When you stop to realize that gambling pays all the state taxes in Nevada, it certainly must exact a heavy toll from the tourists."

"You'd be surprised how much money it puts into California," the pilot said.

"How come?" Mason asked.

"I'd have a hard time keeping this charter service going if it weren't for flights to Las Vegas," the pilot said. "Las Vegas keeps our airlines prosperous, the hotels pay big sums to entertainers—a good many of whom reside in Southern California—and all in all it makes for a good deal of business.

"You also want to remember that very few people lose more than they can afford to lose. It's not big-time gambling in terms of thousands of dollars. Most of the people go there for amusement and they're willing to pay fifty or a hundred dollars to enjoy the thrill of gambling.

"When you come right down to it, I think the people there have a pretty good idea of the amount of business that comes in from Southern California. The Chamber of Commerce had a representative down there checking chartered planes tonight."

"What do you mean, checking chartered planes?" Mason asked.

"Oh, just a routine questionnaire," the pilot said. "They wanted to know how often we made trips to Las Vegas, what percentage of our total business was done on Las Vegas trips, and things of that sort."

"Did they," Mason asked, "inquire as to the name of your passengers, the persons who had chartered the plane?"

"That's right. Wanted to know whether it was a corporation or an individual, whether it was a regular customer or a casual customer."

"Did they ask names?"

"They asked names," the pilot said, "but I thought they were getting a little too personal at that, and told them that it was against my policy to divulge the names of my clients who chartered planes."

Mason glanced at Della Street. "You say this was the Chamber of Commerce?"

"Yes."

"One man or two?"

"It wasn't a man. It was a woman. Not a bad-looking babe."

"Can you describe her?" Mason asked.

The pilot took his eyes from the gauges to look at Mason sharply. "Why?" he asked. "Is something wrong?"

"I don't know," Mason said. "I'm just wondering. I'd like a description of this woman."

"Well, let's see. She was about twenty-nine or thirty, somewhere around in there; a pretty good build, not too tall; nice curves but not chunky. She had blue eyes—well, sort of grayish."

"Blonde or brunette?"

"Brunette."

"Weight?"

"Oh, around a hundred and twelve to a hundred and fifteen—nice."

"How did you know she was from the Chamber of Commerce? Did she show you a card?"

"No. She told me she was from the Chamber of Commerce. She didn't make any bones about it; came right out and told me that they were trying to collect business statistics. She said they wanted to cover chartered airplanes for a month. They were also getting the number of incoming passengers on the regular planes."

"What about automobiles from California?" Mason asked.

"She didn't say anything about that."

"Well, that's all very interesting," Mason said, glancing back from the copilot's seat to where Della Street was putting away her note-book, after having taken down a description of the young woman who had been making the inquiries.

They flew along in silence for some fifteen minutes, watching the stars overhead, the dark bowl of the desert beneath broken by the headlights of automobiles on the paved road below.

"When you come to think of it," the pilot said abruptly, "that's just a little strange. The people who come to Las Vegas by plane are just a fraction of the tourists who come pouring in. Where one comes by plane, a thousand come by automobile. Well, two or three hundred anyway."

"Oh well," Mason said casually, "people do funny things when it comes to gathering statistics."

"They do for a fact," the pilot said. "I guess it's all right, but somehow you've got me thinking."

They landed at the airport in Los Angeles and Mason put through a call for Paul Drake.

"What do you know, Paul?" he asked.

"You're early," Paul said. "I didn't expect to hear from you before two A.M."

"Oh, we're getting along fine," Mason said. "Making progress. Perhaps we'll let you get some sleep. What do you know?"

"Well," Drake said, "Melina Finch, 625 Cypress Avenue, Las Vegas, is twenty-eight years old, a divorcee, brunette, nice figure. She owns a gift shop in Las Vegas but has a young woman who comes in occasionally on buying trips to pick up merchandise. She seems to live well and has some other source of income, believed to be alimony. Her ex-husband is an eastern millionaire."

Mason said. "What about the other Nevada car?"

"That's owned by Harley C. Drexel of 291 Center Street, Carson City. He's a contractor and builder, fifty-five years old, makes a business of buying lots, putting houses on them, selling the house at a profit, buying other lots. Sometimes he has four or five lots and houses going, sometimes he has only one."

"Okay," Mason said. "We may want more details on the Finch woman. We'll skip Drexel for the time being."

"Anything further?"

"Nothing more tonight," Mason said. "Did you have a good dinner?"

"Did I have a good dinner," Drake said. "Boy, I really lived it up. How about you, Perry?"

Mason laughed. "We had a hamburger on the way to the airport and we were so darned busy I forgot all about dinner. I'll bet Della's starving. I expect to remedy my oversight right now. See you tomorrow, Paul."

Mason hung up the phone and turned to Della Street.

"Gosh," he said, "I forgot all about dinner and—"

"So did I," she said, "but my stomach is now reminding me."

"Steak?" Mason asked.

She shook her head. "Ham and eggs for me."

"That sounds good," Mason said. "Come on, let's go."

FIVE

Mason entered his office at ten o'clock in the morning and stood in the door thoughtfully regarding Della Street.

"Della," he said, "when you have been up half the night working, why the devil don't you sleep late in the morning?"

She smiled and said, "Because I can't. I wake up and start thinking of the things that have piled up here at the office and the first thing I know I'm wide awake and up out of bed, taking a shower, cooking breakfast and catching the same old bus."

He grinned and said, "I woke up at the usual time this morning too and started to get up and take a shower, then relaxed and the first thing I knew it was eight-thirty. What's new, Della, anything?"

"Not at the moment. The—"

The phone rang. Della Street picked it up, said, "Yes, Gertie," then after a moment said, "Just a moment. I'll find out.

"Your on-again-off-again client has called the office, asking Gertie if it would be possible to have an appointment with you this morning."

"You mean Adelle Hastings?"

"Yes."

"Let me talk with her," Mason said.

Della Street said, "Just a minute, Gertie. Put her on Mr. Mason's line, will you?"

Mason picked up the phone, said, "Hello?"

Adelle Hastings' voice held a note of urgency.

"Mr. Mason, I simply *must* see you."

"You're here in Los Angeles?"

"Yes."

"How did you get here?"

"I couldn't get to sleep last night. The more I thought of it the more I began to think your idea might be the right one, and if it is . . . I want to see you, if possible before . . . before . . ."

"Before what?" Mason asked.

"Before anything happens."

"What do you mean, happens?"

"Well, if Garvin doesn't keep that ten o'clock appointment this morning Simley Beason will— Well, it will mean something very serious is wrong."

"Probably he's keeping that appointment right now," Mason said.

"That's just the point," she said. "He hasn't shown up at the office as of two or three minutes ago."

"You mean you've been on the phone talking with Mr. Beason?"

"Yes."

"That might not be too good," Mason said thoughtfully. "Where are you with reference to my office?"

"I'm in the parking lot adjoining the building."

"All right," Mason said, "now here's what I want you to do. Come up here right away but don't go to the entrance office. Now, understand that definitely. Don't go to the entrance office. Go to the door marked PERRY MASON—PRIVATE. Knock on that door and Della Street will let you in."

"I'm not to go through the reception room?"

"No."

"And I'm to come right up?"

"Yes."

"I'll be right up," she promised.

Mason hung up the phone and turned to Della Street. "This thing bothers me, Della."

Della, who had been monitoring the telephone conversation, nodded.

"Of course," Mason said, "Adelle Hastings *could* be right about her purse having been stolen."

"And again," Della Street said, as Mason hesitated.

"And again," Mason said, grinning, "she could have come to the office, left her purse and walked away, knowing that someone in the office would find the purse and that the contents would arouse a great deal of interest.

"She had left enough money in the purse so that she could be certain we'd take steps to get in touch with her—even without the gun in the purse we'd have done that."

Della Street waited silently as Mason paused.

"Well?" Mason asked.

She smiled and said, "Go ahead. You're thinking out loud, just using my ears to bounce words off of so you can clarify your own thinking."

Mason might not have heard her. Abruptly he said, "Get Paul Drake on the phone right away, Della. I want to talk with him before Adelle Hastings gets up here."

Della Street's nimble fingers twisted the dial of the telephone with swift efficiency. A moment later she said, "Here's Paul Drake, Chief."

Mason picked up the phone and said, "Paul, this is an emergency matter and I want some fast action."

"You always do," Drake said.

"Hold it," Mason said, "there's no time for kidding. I want you to get as many young women as you can, up to six or seven—no more than that—but six or seven, if possible.

"I want them between twenty-seven to thirty-two. I want them all with good figures, weighing not more than a hundred and seventeen pounds, and not less than a hundred and ten pounds. I want them all to put on heavy dark glasses. You can send one of your operatives down to a drugstore and get a bunch of dark glasses, the biggest and darkest lenses you can find."

"How soon?" Drake asked.

"Right now," Mason told him.

"Have a heart, Perry. I can't—"

"I don't care what you have to pay," Mason said, "I want them. I'm mixed into something that bothers me personally and professionally and I want those women. Probably your receptionist knows some of the girls who are working here in the building who can get away for half an hour or so. Send an operative down to the restaurant. Pick up some of the girls who are having a coffee break. Send someone over to the parking lot. Pick out young women who have parked their cars. Ask them if they want to get twenty dollars for an hour's work. Then give me a ring as soon as you've got them."

"Twenty dollars for an hour's work?" Drake asked.

"Fifty, if you have to," Mason said. "I want results."

"I'm on the job," Drake said. "I'll start with my receptionist. I have a couple of operatives here that are on the loose, and a young chap who can skip down to the drugstore and get dark glasses. You want them big and dark."

"That's right. Big lenses and very dark," Mason said. "We'll give you a ring as soon as we're ready. Now, get this straight, Paul. You have these girls in your office all ready to go, with dark glasses on.

"At the proper time, Della will ring your office and say, 'Paul, this is Della.' That's all she'll say. The minute she says that, you push those girls out into the corridor and have them walk down to the door of my reception room, but tell them not to go in until I come out of my private office with a young woman of that general description, who will also be wearing dark glasses. I'll walk down to the group and we'll all go in together. Got that?"

"Got it," Drake said.

Mason hung up.

Della Street looked at Mason and smiled. "That," she said, "is the advantage of having a detective agency on the same floor of the building in which you have a law office."

Mason nodded thoughtfully.

"The idea is to have something of a line-up?" Della Street asked.

"Exactly," Mason said. "You know Gertie. If I bring Adelle Hastings out into the outer office with dark glasses on and say, 'Gertie, have you ever seen this young woman before?' Gertie will pipe up and say, 'Oh, yes. That's the woman who left her purse here yesterday—Mrs. Hastings. Mr. Mason has your purse in the office, Mrs. Hastings.'

"Human nature being what it is, Gertie by this time remembers only the fact that a well-shaped woman, around twenty-seven or thirty, wearing heavy dark glasses, was in the office and left a purse.

"Now, if anything has happened, and Gertie makes that offhand identification, we might be in trouble."

"What do you think has happened?" Della Street asked.

"If someone has stolen Adelle Hastings' bag and fired two shots from the revolver that was in that bag, almost anything could have happened. And if, on the other hand, Adelle Hastings fired two shots from that revolver and then went to all this trouble to set the stage so that I'd be drawn into the case, you can be pretty damn certain that something *has* happened. She—"

Mason broke off as there was a tapping on the door to his private office.

Mason nodded to Della Street.

Della Street opened the door.

"Good morning, Mrs. Hastings," Mason said. "You must have got up early and had quite a drive."

"I did."

"Where are your dark glasses?"

"Heavens, I don't wear dark glasses except when I'm crossing the desert in the glare of daylight. I never wear them around the city."

"But you do have a pair of dark glasses?"

"Certainly. A person can't drive across the desert between here and Las Vegas without having dark glasses to protect the eyes."

"Quite a glare?"

"A terrific glare."

"What do you do with your dark glasses after you take them off?"

"I put them in my handbag, in a case."

"Were your dark glasses in the handbag that I turned over to you?"

"No."

"Then someone was wearing them."

"Of course."

"You found the empty leather case in your handbag? It was in there when I gave it to you."

"Yes, it's there."

"You now have another pair?"

"Yes. I stopped at a drugstore on the road home yesterday and picked up another pair."

"And you have your purse and handbag with you this morning?"

"Yes."

"Everything was in it, just as I gave it to you?"

"Yes. Why are you asking these questions, Mr. Mason?"

"Let's see your dark glasses," the lawyer said.

She opened her purse, took out a leather case and took out a pair of dark glasses.

"How does it happen those glasses fit the case as though they had been made for it?" Mason asked.

"I have a particular brand of dark glasses that I buy, and I was able to pick up a pair that were the same brand and the same size lenses as those I'd lost."

"So they fitted in the leather case?"

"Yes."

"Suppose there's any chance the clerk who sold you the glasses would remember you?"

"I doubt it. No one sold them to me. I walked into the drugstore, picked out the type of glasses that I wanted, the price was on the glasses and I simply caught the attention of the clerk who was busy waiting on someone else, put the money on the counter, held up the dark glasses and he nodded and waved his hand, indicating it was all right, so I just left the money and walked out. I was in a hurry and he was busy."

"All right," Mason said, "could you find the drugstore again?"

She frowned and said, "I don't know whether I could or not. It was— I think I could. I'd know it if I saw it again. That is, I think I would. It was just another drugstore as far as I was concerned."

"Now, where did you get the money that you used in paying for these dark glasses?"

"I told you my husband gave me five hundred dollars. I told him about someone stealing my purse and he gave me five hundred dollars and told me to get another purse and that would see me home, that probably I'd get all the contents of my purse back except the money. He said that thieves were usually considerate in the matter of driving licenses and things of that sort. He said they didn't like to have incriminating things in their possession. He said there was nothing distinctive about money that could be identified, so they'd take out the money, then put the other things in a big envelope and mail it back to me. He said I'd probably have it by the time I got home."

"All right," Mason said, "let's hear all of your story. What brings you here?"

She said, "You're responsible. I kept thinking over what you said last night. I think something's happened. I'll never feel relaxed again until I know definitely one way or the other."

Mason said, "Would you mind putting on your dark glasses and letting me take a look at you with them on?"

She picked up the glasses and put them on.

Mason regarded her thoughtfully. "Those have very big lenses."

"The biggest they make," she said. "When you're out in the desert, particularly during the summer months, the glare can be absolutely intolerable. You want to shut out as much of it as possible. I'd use goggles, only they are so hot on your eyes. So I've compromised on these glasses. They're the Willikens Glasses, Number 24-X. That's the code number indicating the large lenses and the heavy coloring. They cost ten dollars."

"And tax?" Mason asked.

"No, they're priced at an odd figure so that the ten dollars includes the sales tax. That's true everywhere. No matter what the tax is, the glasses cost ten dollars. The Willikins line is standard. They do a lot of advertising in the slick magazines."

Mason nodded, said, "All right. You called Simley Beason this morning?"

"Yes. It was just before I called you. Simley was worried. He said he had called the house two or three times and that the tape-recording answering service was still on. He said my husband had that important appointment at the office, that when my husband had an appointment of that sort he nearly always arrived ten or fifteen minutes early."

"The appointment hadn't been canceled?" Mason asked.

"No, the man whom my husband was to meet was there in the office waiting. Simley said that if Garvin didn't show up within the next five or ten minutes he was going to drive out to the house to see what the trouble was."

"Would he have a key to the house?" Mason asked.

"He could get one," she said. "There's a key to the house which my husband keeps at the office so that if he's out of town and telephones and wants anyone to go out to the house and get something, the person he sends can pick up the key, and let himself in."

Mason looked at his watch, said, "Then we should know something within the next few minutes. If your husband was called out somewhere he would have left a note and—"

"If he'd been called out," she interrupted, "he would have called the office immediately. I'm afraid he's sick or . . ."

"Or?" Mason prompted, as her voice trailed into silence.

"Or what you thought last night," she said.

Mason consulted his watch, said to Della Street, "Let's give Paul Drake a ring."

Della Street dialed Drake's number.

Mason got on the line and as soon as he heard Drake's voice said, 'Perry, Paul. How are you coming with that assignment?"

"I've got two girls that meet the requirements. One of them is a friend of my receptionist. Another one came from the secretarial agency on the third floor. There's also a secretarial agency on the top floor and I think we can get one or two girls from there. I have an operative up there now."

"The parking lot?" Mason asked.

"No dice down there. At least, so far. I've had an operative down there who hasn't had any luck. Women of that description who put their cars in there are very definitely intent on shopping and, moreover, they're rather suspicious. Even when my operative shows them his identification and tells them that it's a routine matter of just a few minutes' work, they fight shy."

"Even at fifty dollars for an hour's work?" Mason asked.

"Even at that price, they fight shy."

Mason looked at his watch again and said, "I'm fighting the second hand of the watch, Paul. Do the best you can."

"Good Lord," Drake said, "I'm *doing* the best I can. . . . Here comes my man from the secretarial agency on the top floor. He's got two young women with him who answer the description."

"That's fine," Mason said. "Stay with it. Let me know just as soon as you're ready and remember the call that will trigger the thing. Della will just mention her name and hang up."

"I wish I knew what the hell you were getting at," Drake said.

Mason said, "It's probably better that you don't, Paul."

"How soon will you want these girls?"

"Probably within a matter of five or ten minutes," Mason said. "You'll be hearing from me."

Mason dropped the telephone into its cradle, frowned thoughtfully.

"What's all this?" Adelle Hastings asked. "Does this have to do with my case?"

Mason looked at her thoughtfully. "What case?" he asked.

She seemed embarrassed. "Why, I— Well, of course I expect to pay you for your time, Mr. Mason. You'll be compensated."

Mason said to Della Street, "Get Homicide at police headquarters, Della. See if Lieutenant Tragg is in. I'll talk with him, but if he isn't in I'll talk with whoever is in charge."

Della Street nodded, asked for an outside line, then put through the call herself.

"Homicide, please," she said. Then after a moment, "Is Lieutenant Tragg there? Perry Mason calling."

She turned to the lawyer and said, "They're calling him to the phone, Perry."

Mason picked up his phone and nodded to Della Street that she was to monitor the conversation.

Tragg's voice, dry, crisply efficient, came over the line. "Hello, Perry," he said. "Haven't found another body, have you?"

"Would it surprise you?" Mason asked.

"No."

"I don't know *what* I've found," Mason said. "It's something that bothers me."

"That's fine," Tragg said. "Anything that bothers you is certain to bother me. What seems to be the trouble?"

"A client of mine living in Las Vegas, Nevada, lost her purse a couple of days ago; that is, her handbag—the big bag that a woman carries, including lipstick, coin purse, cigarettes and all the rest of the paraphernalia."

"Go on," Tragg said.

"This woman," Mason said, "was Adelle Sterling Hastings, the wife of Garvin S. Hastings. At present Mrs. Hastings has separated from her husband and is residing in Nevada."

"Come on," Tragg said, "get to the point, Mason."

"Yesterday noon while I was out at lunch, and while Della Street was also out at lunch, a woman came to my office—a woman wearing large dark glasses, who said her name was Mrs. Hastings and that she would wait until I returned from lunch. She waited in the outer office for a few minutes and then left rather hurriedly, saying she would return but she never returned.

"Sometime later in the afternoon we discovered a woman's handbag or purse in the office and on making an inventory of that purse we found credit cards, driving licenses, etc., which established the ownership."

"And it was Mrs. Hastings' purse?"

"That's right."

"Then give it back to her," Tragg said, "and— Oh-oh, now, wait a minute, Perry. You're sneaking up on my blind side. Was there by any chance a gun in the purse?"

"There was."

"A permit to carry it?" Tragg asked.

"No. Mrs. Hastings doesn't carry the gun. The last time she saw it, it was in the drawer of a bedstand in her apartment."

"Now, wait a minute," Tragg interrupted. "Had that gun been fired?"

"Twice."

"All right," Tragg said, "come clean, Perry. Where's the corpse that goes with the gun?"

"I don't know that there is any. However, naturally, I'm worried."

"You should be. Where can I find Mrs. Hastings? What's her address in Las Vegas?"

"Her address is 721 Northwest Firston Avenue, but as it happens, she is in my office at the present time. We have been discussing the situation and she feels that something should be done. I felt it would be advisable to notify you, in case you wanted to take a look at the evidence or—"

Tragg's voice was as crisp as a cold lettuce leaf. "All right, Mason, what does she say about the gun having been fired?"

"She knows nothing about it," Mason said. "Her handbag and her keys were stolen, and then the gun was stolen. Moreover, she was not the woman who left the handbag in my office. It was some other woman using her name."

Tragg said, "Why not call the Las Vegas police in case those bullets found a mark in human anatomy somewhere? The body is probably in Nevada."

"That's my thinking," Perry Mason said, "but I thought I should notify you because so many times you complain that I have concealed evidence and that has hampered your investigation."

"It's a crime to conceal evidence," Tragg commented.

"I realize that."

"And that," Tragg said, "is why you're calling me up now. You wanted to clear your own skirts."

"I thought you should know."

"Well, why not call the Las Vegas police?"

"Perhaps I should," Mason said, "but since they're in an entirely different jurisdiction I felt that I would first discharge my responsibility by notifying you."

"All right," Tragg said, "you've notified me. Thanks a lot. I'll keep it in mind. Thanks for calling, Mason. Good-by."

Mason dropped the receiver into the cradle, turned to Adelle Hastings and said, "Tragg will probably be up here just as quick as a siren and the red light on an automobile can get him here. Now, you're going to have to answer questions. If you have told me the truth, answer Tragg's questions fully, fairly and frankly. If you haven't told me the truth, just say that you have no statement to make. Don't, under any circumstances, try to lie to Lieutenant Tragg."

"I understand."

"You weren't the woman who was in this office yesterday?"

"No."

"You didn't leave that handbag here?"

"No."

"You didn't fire that gun?"

"No."

"You left your revolver in your apartment and last saw it there?"

"Yes."

"If you're lying to me," Mason said, "it could very well mean a life sentence or perhaps the death penalty."

"I'm not lying to you."

Mason nodded to Della Street. "Call Paul Drake."

Della Street put through the call, nodded to Perry Mason.

Mason picked up the telephone. "How are you coming, Paul?"

"I've got six women," Drake said, "and as of now they're getting pretty impatient."

"You won't have to hold them much longer. You have dark glasses for them?"

"Yes."

"Big ones?"

"I'll say they're big."

"All right," Mason said, "sit tight. You'll have action within five to ten minutes."

"How long will it take?" Drake asked. "They want to know."

"It won't take over a couple of minutes," Mason said. "Within twenty minutes from now they can go home. Stick around and wait for the signal, Paul. When you get it, act promptly."

Mason hung up and turned to Adelle Hastings. "Put your dark glasses in the case in your handbag. Have them so you can get them at a moment's notice. Now, when Lieutenant Tragg comes here, don't pay the slightest attention to anything that I say. That is, don't let it confuse you."

"What makes you think this officer is going to come here, Mr. Mason? From what I gathered in listening to your end of the telephone conversation there was nothing that he considered very urgent."

Mason said, "I'm putting two sets of two and two together and making two fours, Mrs. Hastings. Then I'm putting those two fours together and making eight."

There was a moment of silence.

"Did you tell Simley Beason that you were going to be here?" Mason asked.

"Yes. I told him I'd call him later but that I was trying to get an appointment with you and he could reach me at your office in case there was anything *real* important."

"Did you tell him—"

Mason broke off as the telephone rang.

Della Street picked up the instrument, said, "Yes, Gertie. . . . Just a moment, please."

Della Street turned to Mason and said, "A Mr. Beason is calling Adelle Hastings."

Mason indicated the telephone instrument to Adelle Hastings. "Want to take the call here," he asked, "or in the law library?"

"Why I'll take it here," she said.

She picked up the telephone, said, "Hello, Simley. This is Adelle. You . . . What! WHAT!! . . . Oh, my God! . . . No. . . . You've . . . you've notified the police? . . . Good heavens. . . . There's nothing I *can* say. . . . This is a terrific shock! . . . Look, Simley,

I'll be in touch with you later. I— Oh, I just can't adjust myself to— Well, thanks for letting me know. . . . Yes, of course you can tell the police where I am, but if it's all right with Mr. Mason I want to go out there right away. . . . I— Well, yes . . . yes, you can tell them. Perhaps that will be best, after all. Thanks for letting me know, Simley."

She hung up and turned to Mason. "My husband," she said, "has been murdered!"

"Surprised?" Mason asked.

"I . . . I guess subconsciously I've been fearing it, Mr. Mason, but the— This information has knocked me for a loop."

Mason said, "You may not have much time. You'd better tell me what he told you."

"He went out there and let himself into the house. My husband was in bed. He'd been shot twice in the head, apparently while he was asleep. He's . . . he'd been dead for some time."

Adelle Hastings started to cry.

Again the telephone rang.

Della Street answered and said to Mason, "Huntley Banner is calling. Do you want to talk with him?"

"Right now," Mason said.

He picked up the telephone, said, "Hello, Banner. This is Mason. What's on *your* mind this morning?"

"About that property settlement," Banner said. "I wanted to check with you and see what the situation was."

"Well, as a matter of fact," Mason said, "Mrs. Hastings is in my office right now. I'm not much of a horse trader, Banner, and I'd like to know just how high you're prepared to go."

"I gave you the figure yesterday."

Mason said, "Look, Banner, when I'm negotiating a settlement of a lawsuit or property matters between husband and wife, I make it an inflexible rule to reject the first offer that is made by opposing counsel."

There was a moment's silence, then Banner said, "Well, what about the second offer?"

"That," Mason said, "depends on the counsel, the amount of the offer, the tone of voice in which it's made and a few other considerations. Now, let's forget this business about what you are prepared to advise your client to do and tell me the most he's willing to do.

Make your top offer and make it now. I'll either give you an ac-
ceptance or a rejection within thirty minutes. If it's a rejection we
won't do any more negotiating. We'll go to court. I want your top
figure."

"You had it yesterday," Banner said.

"No, I didn't," Mason told him. "Give me your top figure now."

"I gave you my top figure yesterday," Banner said. "That is,
that was all I was authorized to offer. I would have to call my client
and get authorization if I'm to go any higher."

"Call your client then," Mason said.

"You're going to be there in your office for a while?"

"Yes."

"I'll call you right back," Banner said.

Mason hung up, looked at his watch and said, "We can expect
Tragg in about three to five minutes. Mr. Banner is going to call me
back as soon as he has conferred with his client."

"You didn't tell him that Garvin was . . . had been . . . ?"

"No," Mason said. "Let's put Mr. Huntley L. Banner to the test
and see just how he works."

There was a period of tense, expectant silence. Then the telephone
rang and Della Street, picking it up, said, "Mr. Banner again."

Mason picked up his own telephone, said, "Yes, Banner."

"I got my client on the phone, Mason. I put the situation up to
him just as you had put it up to me. I told him that you weren't satisfied with the best offer he had authorized me to make, that you were
a fighter and you didn't want to do any horse trading. I told him
that if that was his top offer to let me know and we'd prepare to go
ahead and fight, and if he wanted to make any higher offer under
the circumstances to tell me what it was and to give me his top figure."

"And what happened?" Mason asked.

"Well, when he found that you were going to be representing
his wife he thought the matter over and told me that he'd been giving the whole thing quite a bit of consideration, that he was prepared
to make a figure that would be his top figure and that you could
either accept it or reject it, that it was as high as he was going to go."

"How much was it?" Mason asked.

"It was a rather substantial increase," Banner said. "Frankly, I was
very much surprised, Mr. Mason."

"How much was it?" Mason asked.

"One hundred thousand dollars, payable at the rate of ten thousand dollars a year for ten years plus fifty thousand in his will," Banner said. "And that really knocked me off the Christmas tree because he had told me yesterday that fifty thousand dollars was as high as he would go, no matter what happened."

"You're sure your figures are correct now?" Mason asked.

"Yes."

"You were talking with Hastings?"

"Yes."

"No question about it?" Mason said. "There won't be any backing up or any question that you didn't recognize his voice or were talking with someone else?"

"Look here, Mason, I'm an ethical attorney. I don't do business that way. I've been doing Mr. Hastings' business for some time now. I know his voice and I was talking with Mr. Hastings personally, and that's his top offer. Now, do you want it or not?"

Mason said, "Congratulations on the neatest trick of the week, Banner."

"What do you mean?" Banner asked.

"Your client," Mason said, "has been dead for more than twenty-four hours."

During the silence at the other end of the line, Mason hung up.

Della Street's telephone suddenly exploded into a series of short, sharp rings, Gertie's signal that a police officer had entered the outer office and was on his way in without waiting to be announced.

Mason said to Adelle Hastings, "Here it comes. Get ready."

The door of the inner office opened abruptly and Lt. Tragg stood in the doorway surveying the occupants of the office with skeptical eyes.

"I take it you're Mrs. Garvin S. Hastings," he said, tilting his black hat slightly, studying the shaken client.

"Come in and sit down, Lieutenant," Mason said, "and there's no need leading up to a dramatic period of questioning in which you try to get Mrs. Hastings to betray herself. She knows now that her husband is dead. She received a telephone call from her husband's office manager just a few minutes ago. He advised her that her husband had been shot, and had evidently been dead for some time. He also advised her he was notifying the police. She told him to tell the police she was here."

"So then you called me with this story about the gun and the lost bag?" Tragg asked, his shrewd eyes suddenly shifting from Adelle Hastings to Perry Mason.

"This call," Mason said, "was *after* I had notified you about the bag."

"How long after?"

"Several minutes."

"And I take it you have witnesses to prove it."

"I certainly do. I hope you kept a record of the time my call came in."

"Pretty shrewd," Tragg said thoughtfully, as though talking to himself. "Pretty *damned* shrewd!"

He suddenly shifted his eyes to Adelle Hastings. "All right, Mrs. Hastings, you now know your husband is dead. You know that he's been shot. Do you know that the shots were fired from the gun that was in your purse?"

"No."

"But you weren't too surprised to learn he had been murdered?"

"I was . . . I was shocked."

"Mr. Mason tells me that you lost your handbag or it was stolen."

"It was stolen."

"Where?"

"In Los Angeles. It was stolen from the seat of my automobile. I ran in to a drugstore just long enough to get a package of cigarettes and— Heavens, I didn't have my back turned on the automobile for more than thirty seconds. Someone just grabbed my purse."

"You're certain it was done then?"

"That was the only time it *could* have been taken."

"When did you miss it?"

"Not until I arrived at my house here. I wanted my key. The handbag, change purse and keys were gone. I had to ring the bell so my husband could let me in."

"What else did you have in this bag of yours?"

"Quite a variety of things, such as a woman usually carries. Keys, identification cards, credit cards, lipstick, cigarettes—"

"I thought you said you were out of cigarettes," Tragg interrupted harshly.

"I'm talking about what I usually carry in the bag."

Tragg whirled abruptly to Perry Mason. "You found the bag in your office?"

"Yes."

"Made an inventory of the contents?"

"Yes."

"What about cigarettes?"

Mason kept his eyes steady on Tragg's. "There was a half-filled package of cigarettes in the bag."

Tragg's eyes swiveled back to Adelle Hastings. "That pretty well disposes of your story about being out of cigarettes," he said.

"It does nothing of the kind," Mason interposed. "A thief could have put cigarettes in the bag without the slightest difficulty."

"Then it's your theory that the thief came here?" Tragg asked Mason.

Mason said, "It's my theory that the thief came here. Mrs. Hastings said she wasn't in the office."

"When did you first talk with her?"

"Last night."

"Where?"

"Las Vegas, Nevada."

"You took quite an interest in this handbag, didn't you?"

"There was a fairly good-sized sum of money in it," Mason said.

"How much?" Tragg asked.

"Three thousand, one hundred and seventeen dollars and forty-three cents."

"What time was it when you came here?" Tragg asked Adelle Hastings.

"I didn't come here," she said.

Tragg turned to Mason. "You were out for lunch?"

"Yes."

Tragg turned back to Della Street. "What about you, Della?"

"I also was out for lunch."

"Who was at the desk in the reception office—Gertie?"

"That's right."

"And what does Gertie say?" Tragg asked Mason.

"Gertie described the woman who came in, but it was only a

very general description. Gertie was reading. She only gets the names of clients who come in and then notifies Della Street. Della is the one who takes their addresses and gets an outline of what they want to see me about. Since Della was out for lunch, Gertie simply asked the caller her name."

"And what name was given?"

"That of Mrs. Hastings."

"Let's get Gertie in here," Tragg said. "I'll talk with her myself."

"Now, just a minute," Mason said. "Gertie hasn't seen Adelle Hastings. Mrs. Hastings came in through my private office door. Gertie hasn't seen her."

"So much the better," Tragg said. "We'll see if she can identify Mrs. Hastings."

"Now look," Mason said, "that's not fair."

"Not fair to whom?"

"Not fair to Mrs. Hastings. She can't identify her."

"Why not?"

"When this woman came in the office she was wearing dark glasses. She came in at a time when Gertie was more or less preoccupied, and . . ."

A sudden idea struck Lt. Tragg. He turned to Adelle Hastings. "You've got dark glasses?" he asked.

"Yes."

"With you?"

"Yes."

"Put them on. I want to see how you look."

Mason nodded to Della Street.

Della Street dialed the number of Paul Drake's office, gave the prearranged signal and hung up.

So intent was Lt. Tragg on watching Adelle Hastings open her purse, take out dark glasses and put them on that he didn't pay any attention to Della's call.

"Stand up," Tragg said.

Adelle Hastings stood up.

"That's fine," Tragg said. "Now, that's the way we'll do it. We'll have Mrs. Hastings go out in the corridor through this door. Then she'll walk into the reception office without saying a word. Gertie will be there. *No one will say a word.* Now, if Gertie says, 'You left your purse here yesterday, Mrs. Hastings,' or something of that sort, then we'll have an absolute identification."

"The hell we will," Mason said. "That's no way to make an identification."

"Why not?"

"Gertie knows nothing about there being any question of identification. She would identify anyone who came in the office with dark glasses on. You would yourself. She'll look up, see the dark glasses, and since those will be the most prominent thing that will catch her eye she'll jump to a conclusion and—"

Tragg said, "Do you want to adopt the position that you're going to refuse to allow your client to make a test of this sort?"

"No," Mason said reluctantly, "I don't want to refuse but I don't think it's fair."

"Well," Tragg said, "we're going to do it that way whether you think it's fair or not. Come on, Mrs. Hastings, you're going to go with me."

Mason sighed. "All right, Mrs. Hastings," he said, "I guess Lieutenant Tragg has the whip hand here. Go with him."

Tragg opened the door to the corridor from the outer office, bowed to Mrs. Hastings and said, with his shrewd smile, "You first, my dear."

Adelle Hastings stepped out into the corridor.

Tragg motioned Mason to come along with them.

"I want you to come along, Perry. I don't want you to say anything. Just hang back where you won't be in the way, but I want to be sure you aren't giving anyone any signals. And you, too, Della. I'm going to ask *you* to come along."

It was only after Mason and Della had followed Tragg's instructions that Tragg noticed the crowd of women in front of the door of Mason's reception room.

"Hey, what's all this?" Tragg asked. "You having a delegation call on you or something?"

"We'll go take a look," Mason said.

"First," Tragg said, "we'll just let Mrs. Hastings—"

He broke off as the young women turned at the sound of his voice and Tragg saw they were all wearing dark glasses.

"What the hell!" Tragg said.

Della Street gave a signal and one of the young women opened the door of the reception office and started in.

Tragg hurried down to the group, forgetful at the moment of Mrs. Hastings.

"Here, here," he said, "I want to find out who you folks are and what you're doing here."

Mason said to Adelle Hastings in a low voice, "Hurry along and mingle with the group."

Tragg reached the entrance door just in time to hear Gertie's voice saying, "Oh, hello! What happened to you yesterday? You left your purse and . . ."

Gertie's voice trailed away into amazed silence as she saw that the woman she was addressing was followed by another woman wearing dark glasses, then another and another.

Mason pushed Adelle Hastings along into the group and she entered with another woman.

Tragg forced his way into the office. "Now, just a minute," he said, "just a minute. Gertie, have you seen one of these women before?"

"I— Why, I thought . . . I don't know."

"Now, let's be careful about this," Tragg said. "One of these women came in here yesterday. Which one was it?"

Gertie said, "I thought it was this one," pointing with her finger. "When she came in just now I started to ask her what happened yesterday after she left the office. I wanted to tell her she had left her purse here, but now . . . now I just don't know."

"All right," Tragg said wearily, "line up, you folks. Get in a line there against the wall, all of you."

Mason said, by way of explanation, "This is Lieutenant Tragg of the police. If you'll just do as he says for a moment you won't need to stay any longer than that."

The women lined up.

"Which one?" Tragg asked Gertie.

Gertie said, "I don't know. I thought it was the one who came in first but now I just don't know."

"All right," Tragg said, "you can go, all of you."

Mason glanced meaningly at Adelle Hastings, who was in the line. "All of you can go," he said. "*All* of you."

"Hey, wait a minute," Tragg said, "I want Mrs. Hastings to stay."

"All right," Mason said, "which one is Mrs. Hastings?"

"Don't pull those tricks on me," Tragg said.

"Pick her out if you want her," Mason said.

Tragg said, "You're talking to an officer, Perry. Don't try those tricks."

He moved forward and unerringly placed his hand on Mrs. Hastings' elbow. "*You* stay here," he said.

Mason said, "We'll go back to my office, Mrs. Hastings," and led the way down the corridor.

"What the hell were you trying to do," Tragg said, "make a monkey out of me? Did you think I couldn't pick Mrs. Hastings out of that group? Did you think I'd talk with her without noticing the clothes she was wearing? The color of her hair? The shape of her shoulders?"

"No," Mason said, smiling, "*you* didn't have any trouble picking her out. That's all I needed to convince any jury that the test was a fair one."

Tragg looked at him in exasperation. "Sometimes," he said, "I'm tempted to forget the fact that I like you personally, and take official action against you. I should have known better than to have stuck my head into *that* trap."

"That wasn't a trap," Mason said, "that was a line-up. Any person who is being identified is entitled to a line-up."

"Then why didn't you wait until we could have one down at police headquarters?"

"Because," Mason said, "*you* weren't going to wait for a line-up. You were going to trick Gertie into making an identification on the strength of mental suggestion and a pair of dark glasses."

Mason unlocked and opened the corridor door to his inner office and held it open for Adelle Hastings, Tragg and Della Street to walk through.

"I'm not that naïve," Tragg said. "You had fixed it up with Gertie in advance so that she would identify the first person through that door. If I'd used my head I'd have stopped that bunch of women and seen that Adelle Hastings went through the door first."

"I haven't said a word to Gertie about it," Mason said. "That would be unethical, unprofessional and illegal. I haven't tampered with the witness, I haven't tried to influence her testimony in any way. Gertie is truthful and she will swear to it and what's more, Della will swear to it."

Tragg said wearily, "All right, all right. There was a gun in that purse?"

"There was a gun in that handbag," Mason said.

"Where is it?"

"In my upper right hand desk drawer."

"Well, get it out and— No, you don't, either. On second thought, just open the desk drawer. I'll take charge of it myself."

Mason opened a drawer in his desk, stiffened in amazed surprise, then pulled the drawer all the way out.

"I see," Tragg said. "Another of your little surprises. This one won't work, Perry. I want that gun. This is official."

Mason glanced swiftly at Della Street.

She shook her head.

Mason picked up the office phone. "Gertie," he said, "did you take a gun from a drawer in my office?"

"What? A gun? Heavens, no. I haven't even been in your office all morning. Della was the first one at the office this morning. She knows I haven't been in there."

"Thanks," Mason said, and hung up the phone. He turned to Tragg. "This is beginning to take on a very sinister aspect," he said. "It is now apparent someone is tampering with evidence and trying to frame Mrs. Hastings."

"I see," Tragg said. "Was the missing gun the fatal gun?"

"I don't know," Mason said.

"If it was *not* the fatal gun," Tragg pointed out, "the disappearance was not necessary."

"Why not?" Mason demanded. "In that way Mrs. Hastings is placed in a dangerous situation. Until we have that weapon we can't establish her innocence."

"I see," Tragg said. "And doubtless you feel that until *we* have it *we* can't establish her guilt."

Mason shook his head. "Tragg, do you think I'd be foolish enough to tamper with evidence?"

Tragg smiled. "Let's put it this way. I think you'd be daring enough to do anything you could get away with. Do you have the number of the gun you took from that purse?"

Mason shook his head. "As soon as I saw the gun had been fired I put it in that drawer. I was handling it with a handkerchief but even so I didn't want to have it in my hands. It was a thirty-eight Smith and Wesson."

Tragg turned to Adelle Hastings. "All right, Mrs. Hastings, now we'll have your story. Start at the beginning. When did you see your husband last?"

"I spent the night there."

"Last night?"

"No. The night before last."

"And what were you doing there if you were establishing a residence in Nevada and planning to get a divorce?"

"It was a friendly divorce action. My husband was putting up the money for me to establish my residence and— He was a very warmhearted individual. I think our marriage would have been a success if it hadn't been for other people who interfered."

"Such as whom?" Tragg asked.

"Such as Huntley Banner, for one."

"Who's Banner?"

"An attorney who represented my husband."

"In the divorce action?"

"In everything."

"You hadn't filed for a divorce yet?"

"No, I hadn't established a residence as yet."

"You remained friendly with your husband?"

"Yes."

"How did you happen to come in to see him and spend the night there?"

"He wanted me to come in and talk with him about a property settlement. He said that Banner had some ideas about a property settlement agreement, that those ideas were quite cold-blooded. My husband said that he wanted to do the fair thing, that he wanted me to be satisfied and that he wanted us to part friends."

"And you stayed the night there?"

"That's right."

"In the same bedroom . . . ?"

"No, we had separated. I stayed in another bedroom. I was going to a hotel but Garvin said that was foolish, that he had a house with four empty bedrooms and I might just as well stay there."

"Did you see him in the morning?"

"No."

"The last you saw of him was when he said good night?"

"Yes."

"You knew where his bedroom was, of course."

"Don't be silly, Lieutenant, I was married to the man for eighteen months."

"What time did you leave there?"

"I got up early in the morning and slipped out the back door, got in my car and drove away."

"To Las Vegas?"

"No, not to Las Vegas," she said.

"Where?"

Mrs. Hastings hesitated, said at length, "I left the house. That's all that needs to concern you at this time."

"I want to know *where* you went," Tragg said.

"If you don't mind," Adelle Hastings said, "I won't say anything about where I went after I left the house until I've talked with Mr. Mason about it."

"And if I do mind?" Tragg asked.

"I won't say anything anyway."

Tragg said, "I'm not going to book you for murder at the present time, Mrs. Hastings; and I'm not even going to take you to headquarters for questioning, but I don't want you to leave town. Now, can we have a gentlemen's agreement, Perry. You'll agree to produce this woman for questioning at any time if I don't take her to headquarters now?"

Mason turned to Adelle Hastings. "That means that you can't go back to Las Vegas," he said.

"For how long?" she asked.

"Forty-eight hours," Tragg said.

"All right," she said, "I'll stay here."

"Where will you stay?" Tragg asked.

"I don't know," she said. "I'll go to a hotel."

"And you'll keep in touch with Mason?"

"I'll keep in touch with him."

Tragg turned to Mason and said, "Now, as far as *you're* concerned, Perry, the situation is a little different.

"If you tell me that you put that gun in the drawer in good faith, and that it's disappeared and you don't know what's happened to it, that's all right as far as *I'm* concerned. But I warn you, it isn't going to be all right as far as the district attorney is concerned. Hamilton Burger is going to feel that this is another one of your hocus-pocus flimflams and he's probably going to give you an ultimatum—either produce that gun or go before the grand jury."

"I don't care what Hamilton Burger thinks," Perry Mason said. "I put that gun in this drawer in the desk."

"And that drawer's now empty," Tragg said.

"That's right."

"Any other empty drawers in the desk?"

"No," Mason said. "This is a drawer that I keep for urgent matters that are pending and demanding immediate attention."

"That's very fitting," Tragg said significantly. "That gun is an urgent matter that is pending, and for your information it needs immediate attention."

"I'm going to try to find out about it," Mason said, "but after all, you know the locks on these doors aren't designed to be burglar-proof. They're made so that one master key will open any door on the floor."

"And who has the master key?"

"The janitor, the cleaning woman—frankly, I don't know. I'll have to get in touch with the people in charge of the building and run it down."

"You'd better run it down," Tragg said over his shoulder as he nodded to Adelle Hastings and walked out.

Mason turned to Adelle Hastings. "Did you kill your husband?" he asked.

"No."

"There are some things about your story that are highly fortuitous and rather suspicious."

"I know it," she said. "I can't help it. I told you the truth. You can see what happened. Somebody deliberately framed me. Somebody stole my bag. From the bag this person got the keys to my apartment. Whoever stole the bag went back to my apartment, used the keys to get in the apartment, stole the gun and . . ."

"And used the gun to kill your husband?" Mason asked, as her voice trailed into silence.

"It looks that way."

"Your husband was killed in bed, presumably while he was asleep."

She nodded.

"That means," Mason said, "that the murderer was someone who was in the house, someone he trusted."

"Or someone who had a key to the house," she said.

"All right," Mason said, "you want to direct attention to the purse stealer but you have just told me that your husband kept a key to the house in his office so that if he should telephone and want someone to go and get something out of the house there wouldn't be any hitch."

Again she nodded.

"Now then," Mason said, "that means anyone in the office could have taken a key and gone to the house. How many people are in the office?"

"There must be twenty or thirty people employed there altogether."

"All of whom would have access to the key?"

"No. The key is kept in a closet, and the key to the closet is supposed to be kept in the desk of the manager."

"Then, if your husband should telephone the office and want someone to go out and get some papers or something from his house, the manager would have to go?"

"No, no, not the manager, but the manager would take the key and give it to the person who was being sent out."

"And who would that be?"

"It might be anyone. It might be the office boy, or one of the secretaries."

"And," Mason said, "while that person had the key there's nothing whatever to prevent him or her from stopping in at a key shop and having a duplicate made."

"Yes," she said, "I suppose so, except that the people in the office are presumably people my husband can trust."

"You acted as secretary for your husband before you were married?"

"Yes."

"He was a bachelor?"

"No."

"He had been married before?"

"Yes."

"A widower?"

"No, he was divorced."

"And what happened to the first wife?"

"She was the second wife," Adelle Hastings said. "The first wife died. The second wife— Well, there was a divorce."

Mason regarded her thoughtfully. "The divorce cleared the way for you two to marry?"

"Yes."

"Who got the divorce?"

"The wife."

"Friendly?"

"Definitely not."

"Were you by any chance named as corespondent?"

"Yes."

"Where was the divorce obtained?"

"Nevada."

"Las Vegas?"

"No, Carson City."

"How long ago?"

"About nineteen months."

"And as soon as the divorce decree was signed, you and Mr. Hastings married?"

"Yes."

"Now then," Mason said, "this wife, this divorcee, what about her? Has she forgotten about it and remarried, or—"

"Forgotten about nothing," Adelle Hastings snapped. "She hates the ground I walk on. She'd do anything she could to make trouble. That's the reason I . . . well, I— Well, ever since this business came up of the gun being planted in my bag I've been wondering about her."

"Where is she living now?"

"I don't know."

"What's her name?"

"Hastings. She hasn't remarried."

"I mean her first name."

"Minerva Shelton Hastings, and she's one of the most scheming two-faced little hypocrites I've ever met in my life."

"Was she in love with Garvin Hastings?"

"Minerva Shelton Hastings has only one real love in her life, and that is Minerva Shelton Hastings. She is selfish, cold-blooded, scheming, grasping, cunning, two-faced—"

"Did she love Garvin Hastings?"

"She loved the thought of getting some money."

"And I take it she got some money?"

"She certainly did."

"What was Garvin Hastings worth?"

"Heavens, I don't know. He had properties scattered all over. He must be worth two or three million dollars."

"How much of a settlement did Minerva get?"

"Two hundred and fifty thousand."

"Cash?"

"Spot cash."

"Then if she didn't love Garvin," Mason said, "and she got a good settlement, there's no reason why she should feel bitter toward you."

"Oh, yes there is. She had her hooks into him and if it hadn't been for me she'd have had every cent by this time."

"How?"

"She'd have poisoned him."

"You mean she'd have committed murder too—"

"Mr. Mason, don't misunderstand me. Minerva would stop at nothing. She's ambitious, audacious, cunning, daring and ingenious."

"Then this whole deal is about the type of thing she would have engineered?"

Adelle Hastings nodded.

"But why?" Mason asked.

"To revenge herself on me."

"You mean she'd go to all that trouble and work out that elaborate scheme in order to get even with you?"

"If I were serving a term in prison," Adelle said, "Minerva would be going around with a smile stretching from ear to ear."

Mason said, "There may be more to it than that. Did Garvin make a will while she was married to him, perhaps leaving everything to her?"

"Yes."

"He revoked that will by making a later one?"

"He told me he was going to."

"When?"

"A few days after we were married."

"Now then, in the settlement that was offered me by Huntley Banner," Mason said, "there was a proviso that you were to receive fifty thousand dollars under Garvin's will, as a beneficiary for that amount."

She nodded.

"Therefore," Mason said, "it was intended that your husband would put this in his will."

"Yes, of course. After I had divorced him, he naturally wasn't going to have me as the sole beneficiary."

"But *that* will hadn't been executed as yet?"

"I don't know."

"Do you know if he had executed the other will in your favor?"

"Only that he said he was going to do it. He certainly wouldn't leave the old will in effect."

Mason said, "In any event your marriage to him would invalidate that other will—provided your marriage was legal."

"Of course it was legal. Why do you raise the question?"

Mason said, "It's the curse of the so-called legal mind. You think of *all* the possibilities. Why did your marriage go on the rocks?"

"He . . . I . . . well, he was quite a bit older than I am."

"How much?"

"Fifteen years."

"You knew that at the time you were married."

"Yes."

"And it didn't make any difference then?"

"Mr. Mason, it's very painful for me to have to go into all this, but I was Garvin's confidential secretary. He married Minerva. Gradually he began to find out what a scheming, selfish, cold-blooded, dangerous woman Minerva was. It was only natural that he started confiding in me and that I should sympathize with him and . . . well, I guess we both were swept along into a situation that— Well, where we were both somewhat hypnotized by circumstances and then gradually we began to realize that a sympathetic understanding had been misinterpreted and magnified and made the basis of a romantic attachment. Mr. Mason, I'm not going to talk about this any more. That's a closed chapter in my life."

"You may think it's a closed chapter," Mason said, "but before you get done with this thing the book is going to be opened, that chapter is going to be held up to the attention of the public and the pages are going to be ripped out one by one and spread across the front pages of the metropolitan newspapers."

She looked at him with sheer panic in her eyes, abruptly got to her feet.

"Mr. Mason," she said, "I'm going to a hotel. I'll telephone you and let you know where I am."

"All right," Mason said, "do that. Be sure now you don't try to leave town or conceal yourself in any way, because if you do it will give the prosecution just the ammunition it's looking for. In this state, flight can be construed as an evidence of guilt, and they'd just love to have you start trying to hide.

"That's the real reason that Tragg didn't take you into custody or take you in for questioning. He put you on your honor to stay here in the city, hoping that the pressure would build up and you'd resort to flight, or at least start back for Nevada. Then they'd stop you just before you had crossed the state line and bring you back under arrest, and claim that was evidence of flight."

"And evidence of flight can be used against a person?"

"Yes. It's considered evidence of guilt."

"Thank you for telling me," she said. "I promise you that I won't make a break for it."

SIX

As soon as Adelle Hastings had left Mason's office, the lawyer motioned to Della Street.

"Call Paul Drake, Della," he said. "Ask him to come down here as soon as possible."

Della Street put through the call, hung up the phone, said, "He's coming right away."

Thirty seconds later Paul Drake's code knock sounded on the door of Mason's office.

Della Street opened the door.

"Hi, Beautiful," Drake said, and then turning to Mason said, "Do you want to get any more background on the owners of those two Nevada cars, Perry?"

"I don't know yet," Mason said. "I've got an emergency job for you."

"Such as what?"

Mason said, "I had a gun in this drawer in my desk. Somebody stole it sometime during the night or early in the morning before the office opened up. I want to find out who stole it and I want to get that gun back."

"How important?"

"Damned important," Mason said. "Unless I get it back, I'm going to be charged with suppressing evidence."

"Can they make it stick?"

"I don't know," Mason said. "My story sounds almost as improbable as that of my client, and by the time you put the two stories together we have a fairy tale that a good sarcastic district attorney could shoot as full of holes as a Swiss cheese."

"And I take it," Drake said, "there's a good sarcastic district attor-ney who will be loaded for bear and waiting for the opportunity."

"There is," Mason said.

"Any ideas?" Drake asked.

"I think," Mason said, "it had to be someone who had a pretty good idea of what he was doing. I hate to say this, Paul, but I have a very strong suspicion that my client, Adelle Hastings, is the one who got in here and stole the gun."

"What gives you that idea?"

"She knew where it was, for one thing."

"If you had a gun," Drake said, "there are two places where it would ordinarily be. One of them would be in the safe and the other would be in a drawer in your desk."

"I know," Mason said, "but there's no indication that there was a general search of the office."

"There was no need for a general search," Drake pointed out. "If I'd been looking for a gun I'd have gone to the upper right-hand desk drawer, first thing."

"Well," Mason said, "I don't think it was the job of a professional burglar. I don't think the locks were picked. I think someone got in here, either last night or this morning. Now, no one could have got up to this floor in the evening unless they signed a register in the elevator saying where they wanted to go, and marking down the time. Then they would have to sign out when they left the build-ing."

Drake nodded.

"If it was in the evening," Mason said, "it might have been any one of a number of people. There are a lot of lawyers who come in after dinner for conferences with clients and to look up points in the law library, but somehow I have a hunch it was early this morning. So the first thing to do is to look on the elevator register and see what names are on there for early in the morning."

"How early?"

"Start at two or three o'clock in the morning," Mason said. "Hang it, Paul, start with the first name that's on the register."

"Okay," Drake said, "I'll get busy. It won't take but a few minutes to look at that register. I can bring it down here if you want."

"Go ahead, get it," Mason said. "Now, here's something else. I want you to look up Minerva Shelton Hastings. She was the second wife of Garvin Hastings. His third wife, Adelle Hastings, is my client, and for your information, Garvin Hastings was found dead in bed this morning. He had been murdered. Two shots had been fired into his head while he was sleeping. I'd like to find out something about Minerva's background."

"Okay," Drake said. "I'll start some men working on her and I'll get that register and come right back, if you want."

"I want," Mason said.

Drake left the office, and Mason, frowning thoughtfully, started pacing the floor.

"It darn near has to have been this morning," Mason said half to himself, his eyes on the carpet as he paced the floor.

Abruptly he turned. "Della, do you know when they clean the offices?"

"You mean these offices?"

"Yes."

"On this floor they do it in the morning. On the floor below, at night. The same cleaning women have the job for both floors."

"I had an idea they cleaned them in the morning," Mason said, "because we're in here at all hours of the night and I've never yet run into any cleaning women."

"I think they try to clean here around six in the morning," Della said.

"What about the cleaning women? I wonder if they could be bribed—or victimized."

"Probably victimized," she said. "I doubt if they'd be open to a bribe. They're pretty responsible people."

The lawyer nodded, resumed pacing the floor.

Drake's knock sounded on the door.

Della opened the door.

Drake said, "I think we've struck pay dirt, first rattle out of the box, Perry."

"How come?"

"My detective bureau is open twenty-four hours a day," Drake said. "I keep it open so men who are on the job can have a place to call in and file their reports. Actually we almost never see anyone between ten or eleven o'clock at night and seven-thirty or eight in the morning.

"I try to get in by eight o'clock every morning and I like to have the night operatives have a report on file when I get in, so quite a few of the men come in around six-thirty to seven in the morning, type up their reports, then go out to breakfast."

Mason nodded.

"Now, this morning at six o'clock the register shows there was a Sidney Bell who signed in on the register as coming to my office, but Sidney Bell is a stranger to me. I don't know anyone by that name and I don't have any operative of that name.

"However, the pay-off is that my own office records show that no Sidney Bell came in at six o'clock this morning; in fact there was no one in my office except two or three operatives who came in to type reports."

"We have Sidney Bell's signature there?"

"That's right, right here. Sidney Bell came in at six-o-five and left at six-fifteen."

"And gave his destination as your office?"

"That's right."

Mason said, "Let's find the cleaning woman who does this office, Paul. Get hold of her address and get hold of the elevator operator and see if we can get a description of Sidney Bell."

"I've already done that," Drake said. "One of the assistant janitors runs the elevator early in the morning. He remembers Bell very well. He was a tall man wearing a dark suit and carrying a brief case. Moreover, he was wearing dark glasses. That impressed the assistant janitor. He thought it was pretty early in the morning for a man to be wearing dark glasses."

"Not at all," Mason said. "In this case dark glasses seem to be a universal disguise—and actually it's a damned effective disguise. What about the scrub woman, Paul?"

Drake grinned. "I haven't overlooked that either. Her name is Maude G. Crump. She has a telephone and I saved you a little money there."

"How come?"

"I interviewed her over the telephone. She describes the tall man in the dark suit, wearing dark glasses, who came in with a brief case when she was cleaning your office. He had an air of complete assurance. He said, 'Good morning. I have to go to Arizona on an early plane and want to get some papers. I guess *you* don't mind getting up early in the morning but it's quite a hardship as far as I'm concerned.' "

"Wait a minute," Mason said, "the door to the office would have been closed. They don't leave the office doors open when they're cleaning."

"He tapped on the door, told her he'd forgotten his key, gave her five dollars and a pat on the back. She remembers him as a very fine gentleman."

"Did he tell her he was Perry Mason?"

"Not in so many words, but by his actions he certainly did."

Mason said, "Get Maude Crump on the phone again, Paul. Tell her that if she'd like to make a little extra money she can come in to the office. I want to talk with her. Tell her she may have to wait a couple of hours but that she'll be receiving fifteen dollars an hour."

"Can do," Drake said, "and will do right now. Anything else, Perry?"

"I think that's enough for now," Mason said.

"Okay," Drake said. "Back to the salt mines."

He opened the exit door of the private office and went out.

Mason turned to Della Street. "Now we have a man in the case, Della."

She nodded.

Mason was thoughtfully silent for a few moments, then said, "Did you notice the tone of voice in which Adelle Hastings talked with Simley Beason over the telephone?"

"Gosh, yes," Della Street said. "It was a tone of what you might call warm intimacy."

"Exactly," Mason said. "Now, the man who came up to this office was here in the building only ten minutes. During that time he had to go to the office, tap on the door, get the attention of the cleaning woman, get into the office, get the gun and get out—all within ten minutes.

"Now, of course he may have reasoned the way Paul did, that the gun would be somewhere in my desk. But the way the thing was planned this man had to *know* where the gun was."

"I don't follow you on that," Della Street said.

"If he had anticipated a long search," Mason explained, "he'd have told the cleaning woman he had some work to do and didn't want to be disturbed.

"He didn't do that. He told her he was catching a plane and had stopped in to get some papers. That meant he had committed himself to quick action, a hurried in-and-out affair."

"Gosh, yes!" she exclaimed. "That means he must have *known* no long search was going to be necessary."

"Exactly," Mason said.

"Oh-oh," Della Street said, "I am now beginning to get the full implications."

Mason said, "Call Hastings' office, Della. Let's see if we can get Simley Beason before he goes to lunch."

She put through the call and a moment later said, "Mr. Simley Beason, please. . . . Tell him it's Mr. Mason's office calling—Mr. Perry Mason, the attorney."

She held the phone for a moment, then nodded to Perry Mason and said, "They're calling him. He's coming to the phone."

Into the instrument she said, "Hello, Mr. Beason? This is Della Street, Mr. Mason's secretary. Mr. Mason wants to talk with you. Just a moment, please."

Mason picked up his telephone, said, "Hello, Mr. Beason. I want to have a talk with you as soon as possible. I realize this has been rather a devastating morning as far as you're concerned, but a very embarrassing situation has developed and I feel that you can be of some help to Mrs. Hastings, or perhaps I should say, to the cause of justice and perhaps prevent an injustice being done."

Beason said, "If there's anything I can do, Mr. Mason, I'll be glad to do it. I was very close to Mr. Hastings in his lifetime and of course I saw a good deal of the present Mrs. Hastings while she was employed here, and I'd certainly like to do anything I can to help."

"Could you come up here during the noon hour?" Mason asked.

"Let's see, I was just getting ready to leave for lunch. I— Yes, I could eat later all right. I'll be there."

"Good," Mason said. "I'll wait for you. Thank you very much, Mr. Beason."

The lawyer hung up the telephone and looked at Della Street.

"Well?" she asked.

"It's rather significant," Mason said, "that at no time did he ask me where my office was."

"Of course," Della Street said, "he could look up the address in the phone book."

"And that would take time," Mason pointed out. "He's in a hurry. It would have been very simple to have said, 'Where's your office, Mason?' He didn't ask. I think that means he knew.

"Get Paul Drake on the line, tell him to get Mrs. Crump and ask her to come up here right away. Tell her she may not have to wait over a very few minutes.

"Tell Gertie she can take her lunch hour now, Della, and you can sit out there and watch the outer office. If Beason comes in before Mrs. Crump, bring him right into the office and then go back and wait for Mrs. Crump. Let me know as soon as she comes in."

Della Street nodded. "Sandwiches?" she asked.

Mason grinned. "We're on a Paul Drake diet. Order a couple of hamburgers sent up from the restaurant downstairs."

"With everything?" Della Street asked.

"Everything," Mason said. "Every little bit helps."

SEVEN

Mason's office phone rang and the lawyer, picking up the receiver, heard Della Street's voice saying, "Mr. Simley Beason in the office. He says you're expecting him."

"Show him in," Mason said.

A moment later Della Street opened the door and a tall man of about thirty-five with wavy, dark hair, dark intense eyes and wearing a dark suit, came forward with his hand outstretched.

"Mr. Mason," he said, "I'm very glad to meet you."

"It's my pleasure," Mason said, gripping the hand cordially. "Won't you be seated?"

Beason settled himself in the overstuffed leather chair.

Mason said, "I want some information. I need it fast and i think you're the person to give it to me."

"I'll do anything I can."

"Of course I understand that as an employee of Hastings' far-flung business enterprises you have a lot of responsibilities and this is probably a very bad day for me to take up any of your time. Nevertheless, I consider the matter of some importance.

"I also realize that you have a loyalty to the dead man and to the business, but I think you're essentially fair and feel certain you won't mind my asking a few questions."

"Go right ahead," Beason said. "I'll be glad to do what I can." And then added meaningly, "In the brief time that I can spare from the business today. You'll understand I've had to answer a lot of questions."

"I understand," Mason said. "I'll try to be as brief as possible. You've been working for the Hastings Enterprises for how long?"

"About twelve years."

"You knew the first Mrs. Hastings?"

"Yes."

"She died?"

"Yes."

"And the second Mrs. Hastings?"

"That's Minerva Hastings," Beason said. "Yes, I know her."

"Would you care to express an opinion?" Mason asked.

Beason looked at the carpet for a moment, then raised his eyes to Mason's. "No," he said.

"And, of course you know Adelle Hastings."

"Yes."

"Would you care to express an opinion?"

"I have known Adelle since she came to work for the organization," Beason said. "She is a very fine woman. She was Mr. Hastings' secretary before he married her."

"There was some sort of a scandal, I believe?" Mason asked. "Wasn't she named as corespondent?"

Beason started to say something, stopped, stroked the angle of his jaw with the tips of his thumb and forefinger, said, "I wouldn't care to be quoted, Mr. Mason, but I can give you the situation in a nutshell. The first Mrs. Hastings was a very fine woman. When she died Hastings was lonely and he thought of women and of marriage in terms of his first wife. He met Minerva. It never occurred to him that marriage with her would be radically different from what it had been with his first wife. He was a pushover."

"You mean Minerva was the aggressor?"

"I didn't say that," Beason said.

"Not in so many words," Mason said.

"Let's leave it the way I said it."

"Go ahead. Tell me about Adelle."

"Mr. Hastings' thoughts of marriage were in terms of the happiness he had enjoyed with his first wife. Reality gradually dawned on him after he married for the second time.

"Adelle was his secretary and— Well, we could all of us see that Mr. Hastings was suffering, suffering tremendously. I think he con-

fided in Adelle and they were together a great deal. A close friendship ripened into love."

"And of course Minerva was furious," Mason said.

Simley Beason looked up quickly. "Not necessarily," he said.

"What do you mean by that?"

"There is, of course, a possibility that Minerva did not regard her
marriage to Hastings as a permanent alliance, looking upon it as a
means of financial advancement.

"Mind you, Mr. Mason, I am not saying that is the case but if it
had been the case, then of course she would have looked upon the
situation which developed with a great deal of satisfaction because
it would give her an opportunity to get a divorce, to pose as the
aggrieved woman, to put Garvin Hastings in the wrong and to collect a large sum by way of alimony."

"Were there indications that this might have been the case?" Mason asked.

"About the time Mr. Hastings began to develop a warm friendship for Adelle, Minerva Hastings went back east to visit relatives
and— It seemed to persons around the office that Minerva deliberately closed her eyes and created all sorts of opportunities for Garvin Hastings and Adelle Sterling to be together."

"And then?" Mason asked.

"Oh, then there was the usual blow-up, the recriminations, the
negotiations for a property settlement, and it wound up by Minerva going to Carson City, Nevada, establishing a six weeks' residence and getting a divorce. Adelle Sterling and Garvin Hastings
were married within a week of Minerva's divorce."

"And what happened to Minerva?"

"She's around."

"Do you ever see her now?"

"No, but I talk with her on the phone from time to time. You
see, she secured a rather large sum of cash by way of settlement and
also some properties that Mr. Hastings had acquired, and of course
I was familiar with those properties. Minerva Hastings rings me
from time to time to ask questions about them."

"What is her manner?"

"I don't think she likes me at all. Her favorite is Connely Maynard
who is the general manager of the Enterprises. They have known
each other for some time."

"How long have they known each other?"

"For some time."

"Before her marriage to Hastings?"

"I think they had some friends in common."

"And how well do they know each other now?"

"I don't know."

"Would you care to speculate as to whether there is anything more than friendship involved?"

Beason hesitated a moment, then said, "No. Speculation in such a matter would be profitless."

"Where does Minerva Hastings live now?"

"She alternates her time between here and friends she formed in Nevada while she was establishing her residence there. Minerva is restless. She comes and goes."

"All right," Mason said, "I want your opinion. Do you think she's in love with Connely Maynard?"

Beason thought for a moment, then said, "She's in love with power, she's in love with money, she's in love with herself. All other emotions are secondary."

Mason said, "You know generally what happened here yesterday. Some woman stating she was Mrs. Hastings left her handbag in the office and there was a gun in the handbag."

"So I understand," Beason said.

"This woman was wearing dark glasses which made it a little difficult to identify her."

"Yes. I understand that."

"Do you think there is any chance this woman could have been Minerva Hastings?"

Beason was thoughtful. "Minerva Hastings," he said, "is very resourceful, very daring, very shrewd. If she engaged in any activity of that sort it would have been well planned—down to the smallest detail."

"Apparently," Mason said, "this was well planned, down to the smallest detail."

Beason said nothing.

The phone rang sharply.

Mason picked it up and Della Street said, "Mrs. Crump is in the office."

"I see," Mason said. "I think we had better proceed."

"That means I'm to send her in?"

"Yes," Mason said.

Mason opened the drawer of his desk, handed a pair of dark glasses to Simley Beason.

"Would you," he asked, "mind putting these on?"

"Why?" Beason asked.

"I just want to see if it would make a difference in your appearance."

Beason hesitated a moment, then put on the dark glasses.

Mason regarded him critically.

The door from the outer office opened and Della Street said, "Mrs. Crump."

"Oh, hello, Mrs. Crump," Mason said, "would you mind coming in and being seated for a moment?"

Mrs. Crump, a chunky woman in her fifties, came marching forward.

Simley Beason hastily snatched at the dark glasses.

Mrs. Crump turned to look at him, said, "Why, what happened, Mr. Mason? Didn't you go to Arizona after all?"

Beason smiled weakly, nodded his head toward Mason and said, "That's Mr. Mason. I'm Simley Beason."

"Why, you— Aren't you . . . ? Why, you're the one who—"

"I think he is the one, Mrs. Crump," Mason said. And turning to Beason, said, "I'd like very much to get a complete story of what you were doing in my office this morning shortly after six o'clock, and what happened to the revolver you took out of the upper right-hand drawer of my desk."

Mason smiled at Mrs. Crump and said, "That's all, Mrs. Crump. That's all we need you for at the moment. If you'll return to the outer office, Miss Street, my secretary, will see that you're given a check for your services. I hesitated to bother you but—"

"That's all right, that's all right," she said. "I'm only too glad to do anything I can."

She gave Beason a look of obvious distaste, then turned and lumbered from the office.

Mason tilted back in the swivel chair, lit a cigarette, extended his hand for the dark glasses and sat silent.

The pressure of continued silence was too much for Beason.

"All right," he said, "I suppose it was a clumsy attempt. I did what I could to aid Adelle."

"Just how friendly are you and Adelle?" Mason asked. "What *is* the relationship?"

"There's nothing improper, if that's what you mean," Beason said, "but I— Damn it, Mason, I . . . I suppose I've trapped myself. I suppose I'm in one hell of a predicament right now."

The lawyer sat at his desk saying nothing, waiting for Beason to assume the conversational initiative.

"All right," Beason said, "I can tell you because you know it anyway. I think the world of Adelle Hastings. I . . . I love her."

"How long have you felt that way?" Mason asked.

"I was drawn to her from the first minute she entered the office. I won't say it was a case of love at first sight, but I was very much interested in her, very much fascinated by her."

"Every take her out on a date?" Mason asked.

Beason shrugged his shoulders. "What chance does an employee stand when the boss is falling in love?"

"It depends," Mason said. "It might depend a great deal on the woman."

"I don't think Adelle realized how I felt toward her."

"Does she realize now?" Mason asked.

"I don't know. I've never said anything that would give her that impression, but— Well, she's been very friendly, very considerate, and very nice to me."

"And she told you what had happened about the handbag and the gun?"

"Yes. After you left Las Vegas I became very much concerned about the telephone call Adelle had made while you were there, so I called her back and asked her to tell me what the trouble was."

"And she did?"

"Not over the telephone. She said she was going to drive in."

"So you met her sometime in the small hours of the morning?"

"At five o'clock," Beason said. "We had breakfast together. Good Lord, what am I saying? I'm putting my neck in a noose and hers right along with mine. I never thought any of this would come out."

"Lots of things come out in a murder case," Mason said.

Beason said, "I was only trying to help. Apparently I didn't do such a good job."

"You certainly didn't," Mason said. "Not only for Adelle Hastings, but you've put *me* on the spot. How did you know where to find that gun?"

"Adelle told me what you had done with it."

"Then, *she* knew you were going to come up here and get it?"

"Heavens, no! She didn't have the slightest idea. She told me her story. She asked me what to do. She had no idea what I intended to do."

"Did she tell you that she had been the one who left the bag in my office?" Mason asked.

"No, no! Don't you understand? That's the reason I became interested and . . . in doing what I did. She said very definitely that her handbag had been stolen, that there was no gun in it when it was stolen, and that then the gun was found in the handbag which had been left in your office by a woman who claimed she was Adelle Hastings. So right away I knew she was being deliberately framed."

"You hadn't discovered the body of Hastings at that time?"

"I hadn't discovered the body, no. However, I had done everything but that. I put two and two together and came to the conclusion that something had happened . . . that some crime had been committed with that gun and that there was a deliberate, determined attempt to blame it on Adelle."

"So you were going to do everything you could to see that Adelle was kept in the clear."

"Let's put it this way, Mr. Mason. I felt that someone was desperately trying to get Adelle in a lot of trouble and I felt that I'd . . . well, that I'd throw a few monkey wrenches in the machinery."

"All right," Mason said, "where's the gun now?"

"I've got it where no one is going to find it."

"I'm going to find it," Mason said.

"What do you mean by that?"

"I'm going to get that gun and turn it over to the police," Mason said. "Can't you understand? You've left me in the middle. I've told the police my story about the gun. I had to. The gun is evidence. I'm an attorney. I can't conceal evidence. You're a citizen. *You* can't conceal evidence. You would put yourself in the position of being an accessory after the fact. If you beat that, you might be convicted on a charge of concealing evidence. I want you to get that gun and I want you to get it right away."

"And then you're going to turn it over to the police?"

"Certainly I'm going to turn it over to the police."

Beason sighed wearily. "All right," he said. "I guess I know when I'm licked. May I use the phone?"

"Right here," Mason said, indicating the telephone. "Just press that button and it will give you an outside line."

Beason took the phone, pressed the button and waited until the light came on and dialed a number.

"Hello," he said, "I want to talk to Rosalie."

Beason waited for a few moments, then said, "Hello, Rosalie? This is Simley Beason. I want you to do something very important for me right away. I'm at the office of Perry Mason, the attorney. I want you to go to my locker and in there you'll find my golfing clothes and a golf bag full of clubs.

"Take the golf bag out, lift the clubs out of the golf bag, turn it upside down and a package will fall out—a package that is done up in brown paper and that has a label on it stating that the contents of this package were taken from the desk drawer in Perry Mason's office at six o'clock this morning. You'll find the address of Mason's office on that label, and you'll find my signature on it. That tag is fastened to the brown paper with tape and the package is sealed.

"I want you to bring that package to me at Mr. Mason's office just as fast as you can get here. Take a taxicab. You can join me in Mason's office and I'll drive you back. Have you got that?"

Beason listened for a few moments, then said, "Good girl. I'll be waiting here."

Beason hung up the telephone and said to Mason, "I don't suppose I need to tell *you* how satisfactory it is to have a good, loyal secretary, but it's a wonderful feeling. I've been putting up with some pretty mediocre secretaries for a while and then Rosalie Blackburn came along and it's made all the difference in the world. You only need to tell her something once and she gets it and gets it right."

"Why did you go to all the precaution of sealing that package and putting a label on it?" Mason asked.

"I did it to protect Adelle Hastings. If anything should happen to me I didn't want anyone to find that package and think that Adelle had been responsible for putting it there."

"What do you mean, in case anything should happen to you?"

"Oh, I'm not morbid, Mr. Mason. I just recognize the fact that these days a person can get killed in an automobile accident just as easy as not, and— Well, life is full of risks, that's all."

Mason regarded him narrowly. "That's the only reason you took all those precautions?"

"Well, I wanted to . . . I wanted to have the thing done right."

"Did you," Mason asked, "write down the number on that gun when you had it in your possession and before you wrapped it?"

"No. Why should I have done that?"

"To see no one changed guns on you and perhaps substituted the fatal gun for Adelle's gun."

"No, I didn't take the number, but I wrapped it in tissue paper, then in heavy brown paper, sealed the paper with tape, wrote my name across the seal and labeled the package."

Mason said, "You may have undone the very thing you were trying to do."

"What do you mean?"

Mason said, "Hastings was murdered. It was a cold-blooded deliberate murder. You don't shoot a man in his sleep in the heat of passion. When a man is lying in bed and you sneak up alongside of him while he is asleep and pull the trigger, you are committing a premeditated, planned murder."

Beason nodded.

"And then when you take the precaution of shooting him twice in the head, you want to be very, very certain that he is dead."

Beason shifted his position, then rather reluctantly nodded his head.

"So we are dealing with a cold-blooded murderer," Mason said, "a person who is shrewd, resourceful, selfish and probably ingenious as the devil.

"Now then, Hastings had his house locked. There is no indication that anyone forced any of the windows. Therefore the police reasoning will be that whoever entered the house had a key. Now, as I understand it, there were two outside keys to the house. One of them was in the office, so that if Hastings wanted anyone to bring papers to the house, or get anything from the house in his absence, he could telephone and have it done. The other key was in the possession of Adelle Hastings. Now, how about a possible third key? What about Minerva, did she keep a key?"

"No, she sent her key in with a very bitter letter."

"How do you know?"

"Mrs. Hastings showed me the letter."

"What was in it?"

"Oh, it was an act. She was laying the foundation for a good property settlement. She said that she felt like an old shoe, that he had been proud of her when she was new and then he had discarded her and thrown her out on the trash heap."

"She got a good property settlement?" Mason asked.

"I considered it a very good property settlement. She didn't."

"What attorney negotiated it, the Nevada attorney?"

"No, she and Hastings worked it out by themselves."

"That's rather unusual," Mason said.

"Hastings is rather unusual in matters of that sort. He has a banker's way of looking at things. He feels your first mistake is your best mistake and that, in the long run, if you have to pay you had better pay and pay cheerfully."

"All right," Mason said, "we'll look at it this way. Someone who is very ingenious, very vindictive, very ruthless, has a key to the Hastings house—or was able to get a key to the Hastings house.

"Since Adelle is my client and your friend, we'll leave her out of it for the moment. Therefore the key was probably the key that is kept in the office. Now then, if Adelle's gun was not the murder weapon, but you took that gun up to the office and somebody knew where you had put it, switched guns and put the fatal gun where you left Adelle's gun, you can see what the situation would be."

Beason frowned; there was a trace of panic in his eyes, but he said, "I'm afraid, Mr. Mason, that you're doing a lot of negative thinking, if you don't mind my saying so. After all, I put that gun in a sealed package. Nobody can tamper with it without having it appear that the package was tampered with, and I took particular pains to conceal it where no one would ever look for it."

"All right," Mason said, "we'll—"

The telephone rang a quick, short ring.

Mason picked up the receiver, said, "You still out there at the board, Della?"

"I am," she said. "Gertie should be back any minute. You now have a call from Mr. Huntley Banner, who says it's very important. Do you want to take it?"

"I'll take it," Mason said. "Put him on."

Della Street switched the call onto Mason's line.

"Hello, Banner," Mason said. "What's on your mind?"

Banner said, "I wanted you to know that I rather resented the way you took advantage of me on that phone call."

"How did I take advantage of you?"

"You knew that I would react by telling you I'd been in touch with my client."

Mason said, "I had no idea you would make a false statement."

"I'm not particularly keen about the way you handled it," Banner said, "but I certainly did walk into a trap."

"You called me up simply to tell me you didn't like it?" Mason asked.

"No, I called you up on another matter, but I think you'd better understand I don't like to have people play games with me."

"What's the other matter?" Mason asked.

"I am assuming," Banner said, "that Adelle Hastings will be your client and that you will be representing her."

"And so?" Mason asked.

"She hates the ground I walk on," Banner said. "Now, there's very definitely a big estate to be probated. I'm fully familiar with all of Hastings' affairs, and I'd logically be the attorney to take charge of the estate. But of course under the circumstances I know that I don't stand a ghost of a chance if Adelle Hastings is in the saddle.

"I've just received a call from Minerva Hastings. In case you don't know it, that's Garvin Hastings' divorced wife. She wants me to represent her, and I'm going to do it. I just wanted you to know."

"Represent her in what?" Mason asked.

"In all matters in connection with the estate."

"Wasn't there a property settlement and a divorce?" Mason asked.

"I'm not tipping my hand right at the moment," Banner said, "but as an attorney you are doubtless familiar with the provisions of our law that when a man has been murdered, the murderer cannot inherit from the victim regardless of what legal claim that person might have on the estate."

"I see," Mason said. "So now you're going to prove that Adelle Hastings is guilty of murder, is that it?"

"I'm going to sit back and let the police do the proving," Banner said. "I'm representing Minerva Hastings. There's no law against it, it's not unethical, and I'm going to take all steps which may be necessary to protect her interests. I'm just doing you the courtesy of letting you know."

"All right," Mason said, "you've let me know."

"And for your information," Banner said, "the more I think of it the less I like that trick you played on me."

Mason said, "I wanted to find out just how honest you were."

"All right," Banner snapped. "I hope you're satisfied."

"I am. I found out."

"I didn't mean it quite that way," Banner said.

"I did," Mason told him, and hung up.

He turned to Beason and said, "That was Mr. Huntley L. Banner, telling me that he was going to represent Minerva Hastings. Apparently Minerva got on the job rather rapidly, all things considered."

"And he's going to represent *her?*" Beason asked.

"That's what he says."

"I wouldn't doubt that he's been representing her all along."

"What do you mean by that?"

"Well . . . I guess— Well, I guess I haven't any solid, substantial proof that I could rely on so I'd better not say anything."

"You did, however, have some reason for making that statement," Mason said.

"I've never trusted Banner," Beason said.

"He doesn't seem to inspire confidence," Mason observed dryly, "yet Hastings seemed to turn over everything to him."

"I don't think it was Hastings' fault entirely. It was Connely Maynard who is responsible for that. He's the one who consulted Banner when Hastings was out of town and a legal matter came up and then gradually Banner moved in on the whole deal."

"Perhaps you'd better tell me a little more about Connely Maynard," Mason said, "and just what makes you so suspicious of Huntley Banner."

"I shouldn't be talking to you like this," Beason said. "You're managing to turn me inside out."

"You want to help Adelle, don't you?"

"Yes."

"I'll tell you this much," Mason said, "she's in a spot. I can't help her unless I have the information I need, and right at the moment I don't know anybody who's better qualified to give me information than you. Now, what about Maynard?"

"Maynard," Beason said, "is the second in the chain of command. He's above me. He'll probably be the one who takes charge of things now that Hastings is dead— That is, until you can get the necessary papers so that Adelle can move in."

"The business is a corporation?" Mason asked.

"No, it's a one-man concern."

"Then nobody can step in and take charge until there's a court order," Mason said.

"I suppose so," Beason said dubiously, "but Maynard is the thrusting, pushing type, the aggressive sort, and he has a lot of very detailed information."

"You have a lot of detailed information yourself, don't you?"

"Yes."

"Do you know as much as he does, as many of the details?"

"I don't think so, no. I have a pretty good grasp of the details of the business, however."

"All right," Mason said, "let's get back to Banner. What's your feeling about him?"

Beason hesitated for a moment, then asked, "Have you ever met Elvina Mitchell, Banner's secretary?"

Mason's eyes snapped into hard focus. "Yes," he said. "What about her?"

"She is a close friend of Connely Maynard. She's been friendly with him for some time."

"I thought perhaps she was palsy-walsy with her boss," Mason ventured.

"She may be, but I don't think so. I think she's all wrapped up in Connely Maynard."

"Go ahead," Mason said. "Do some more talking."

"Well, she naturally wanted to have Banner handle Hastings' business. Hastings shopped around with two or three different lawyers when certain matters came up, but usually Hastings liked to handle things himself and he didn't have very much legal business.

"Then a deal came up when Hastings was out of town and Maynard got Hastings on the phone and told him he thought he'd better see an attorney, and Hastings told him all right, to go ahead. So Maynard went right to Banner and from that time on Banner has been moving into the legal end of the business, pushing himself in in every way possible, telling Hastings that he mustn't do this, that, or the other without consulting an attorney, that he could get in serious difficulties if he acted without legal advice. Finally he changed Hastings' method of doing business. In place of doing what he thought was right, and then making settlements when he had to, Hastings got so he was going to Banner more and more."

Mason said thoughtfully, "That makes a very interesting situation. And now Banner is going to be representing Minerva. I wish you had left that gun in my desk drawer."

"It's just the same as in your desk drawer. It's all wrapped up and sealed and my name is written across the seal and I can go into court and swear that it's the same gun and that it hasn't been tampered with."

Mason said, "Let's hope it hasn't been tampered with."

Della Street came in from the outer office and said, "Gertie's back."

Mason said, "Della, get papers together for a petition for letters of administration on the estate of Garvin S. Hastings. We'll have Adelle Hastings file the petition."

"Wasn't there a will?" Della asked.

"I don't know," Mason said. "If there was one Huntley Banner has it, and Huntley Banner is now representing Minerva Hastings. So the situation is getting complicated. Let's get the papers all ready for Adelle Hastings' signature right now, Della, because events may start moving rather swiftly. We'd also better get a petition for Adelle as a special administratrix in order to conserve the estate."

"Isn't that action rather abrupt?" Beason asked. "Don't they usually wait until after the funeral?"

"This isn't a usual case," Mason said. "I have an idea we're going to have to work fast. . . . Della, just as soon as Adelle lets us know where she's staying, get her signature on those petitions."

"I know where she'll be staying," Beason said. "At the Freestone Hotel Apartments."

"That's her usual place to stay when she's in town?"

"Yes."

"Night before last she stayed at the Hastings residence," Mason said.

"That's right. Garvin insisted that she do it. To tell you the truth, Mr. Mason, I think Garvin Hastings was lonely and had begun to realize what a tragic mistake he had made in asking Adelle to terminate the marriage. I think he wanted to make up."

"And were you simply going to sit back on the sidelines?" Mason asked.

Beason said, "I've been sitting on the sidelines for many months, Mr. Mason. I guess that's my trouble. But I wanted Adelle to do what was best for *her*. . . . I would have felt diffident about competing with five million dollars."

Mason regarded him thoughtfully. "You feel diffident, period," he said. "Perhaps you'd better get over that and start fighting for what you want. Diffidence is a virtue women fail to appreciate."

Beason lowered his eyes. "I love her so much I wanted her to do what was to her her best interests. Hastings could give her things I couldn't."

EIGHT

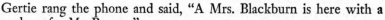

Gertie rang the phone and said, "A Mrs. Blackburn is here with a package for Mr. Beason."

"Just a minute," Mason said. He turned to Beason. "Mrs. Blackburn is out there," he said, "with a package for you. Shall I have her come in or do you want to talk with her privately?"

"No, no, have her come in."

"I gathered she was unmarried from the way you talked. She gave the name of Mrs. Blackburn."

"No, she's been married. It's rather a tragic history."

"A widow?" Mason asked.

"Divorced. Her husband just failed to come home one night and she never saw him after that."

"So she went to Nevada?"

"That's right."

"Las Vegas?" Mason asked.

"Carson City."

"How long ago?"

"Shortly before she came to work for us, about a year, I think."

Mason said, "Tell her to come in, Gertie. Della will meet her at the door."

Della Street moved to the door which communicated with the short passageway leading to the reception room and a moment later a dark-haired, dark-eyed young woman stood on the threshold.

"Come in," Mason said.

Rosalie Blackburn flashed him a swift glance, then her eyes

swung to Simley Beason. She lowered her eyes at once, hesitated, flashed Beason another glance, then entered the room.

Simley Beason got up from his chair, extended his hand for the package, said, "Rosalie, this is Mr. Mason, the famous attorney. You've heard a lot about him and read a lot about him— What the devil! *What's happened to that package!*"

"That was the way it was when I took it from the golf bag," Rosalie said.

"Why, the thing is all unwrapped. The whole paper has been cut open," Beason said. "You can see the gun— Rosalie, *you* didn't do this, did you?"

"No, sir. I brought it to you just the way it was."

"And my locker was closed and locked?"

"That's right. I got the key from the top left-hand drawer in you desk, where you keep it."

"Well, *that's* something," Beason said.

He started to unwrap the package, then hesitated and said, "Rosalie, if you'll go into Mason's outer office and just sit down and wait I'll be with you in a few minutes and drive you back."

"Thank you," she said, flashed a vague smile and turned and hurried from the office.

"As your secretary," Mason asked, "does she have rather an inordinate curiosity as to your affairs?"

"She's very efficient," Beason said, "but if you're asking me if she opened that package I'd stake my life that she didn't."

Mason said, "You may be staking just that.

"Della, put those wrappings in a carton and seal up the carton so we can get them at any time we may need them, and be careful not to get any more fingerprints on them than is necessary."

"Can you *get* fingerprints from paper?" Beason asked quickly.

"By using a new process, you can," Mason said. "Sometimes the fingerprints are startlingly clear and they last almost indefinitely. It's a different process from the usual type of latent fingerprint developing where you use powder and the powder sticks to the moisture of the latent fingerprints. These prints are the result of amino acids and are brought out by chemical, rather than a physical process."

"Gosh, I didn't know you could get fingerprints from paper,"

Beason said. "Of course my fingerprints are all over it and I presume Rosalie's will be all over it."

"I would certainly suppose so," Mason said. "You both seem to have handled it enough."

Della Street opened a closet door, took out a carton in which law books had been shipped. Carefully picking up the outer wrapping paper by the edges, she put it in the carton, then using equal care, removed the inner layer of paper and disclosed the blued steel revolver.

Mason bent forward, inserted a pencil in the barrel of the gun, lifted it gingerly to the desk, placed it in the drawer.

"Now," he said, "we'll call Lieutenant Tragg and tell him that the gun which I mentioned to him *had been* misplaced but I now have it."

"Had been misplaced covers quite a bit of territory," Della said.

"Exactly," Mason told her. "Give him a ring and use those words —the gun had been misplaced."

Mason said to Beason, "I don't think we need to detain *you* any longer, Beason. Lieutenant Tragg of Homicide is very efficient. He may get up here within the next few minutes. He'll undoubtedly be very anxious to get hold of that gun."

"Meaning that there's no longer any necessity for me to be here?" Beason asked.

"Meaning that it would be well for you *not* to be here," Mason said.

"You're going to try to protect me?"

"Hell no! I'm going to protect my client first," Mason snapped, "and after that I'm going to protect myself. You've stuck your neck into this thing and it's up to you to protect yourself."

NINE

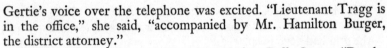

Gertie's voice over the telephone was excited. "Lieutenant Tragg is in the office," she said, "accompanied by Mr. Hamilton Burger, the district attorney."

"Send them in," Mason said, and nodded to Della Street. "Do the honors, Della."

Della Street, with something of a flourish, opened the door connecting the passageway to the outer office.

Hamilton Burger and Tragg came striding into the room.

There was something of an apologetic, whimsical smile on Tragg's face, but Hamilton Burger's face was grim and official.

"Well, well, how do you do, gentlemen?" Mason said. "I suppose you're here in regard to the gun. Won't you sit down?"

Hamilton Burger said, "We're here in regard to a number of things. Most of those things have to do with that gun. Now, just what are you trying to pull here?"

"I'm trying to co-operate with the police," Mason said.

"A little of your co-operation goes a long, long way," Burger said, and nodded to Tragg.

"Where *is* the gun?" Tragg asked.

Mason opened the right-hand desk drawer.

Tragg said, "Why wasn't it in that drawer when I was here before?"

"It's a long story," Mason said.

"You said over the telephone that you had misplaced it."

"I beg your pardon," Mason said, "I think my secretary told you the gun *had been* misplaced."

"By whom?"

"Now, that's a long story," Mason said. "I'm debating with myself whether to tell you or not."

"Well, you'd better tell us," Hamilton Burger said, "because I'm doing a little debating myself. I'm going to have you before the grand jury and I don't know whether to try and get you for being an accessory after the fact on a murder charge or concealing and tampering with evidence."

"Under those circumstances," Mason said, "perhaps I had better *not* tell my story until I appear before the grand jury."

Burger said to Tragg, "Can you check that gun for fingerprints?"

"You seldom find fingerprints on a gun," Tragg said. "Sometimes on an automatic you get a thumbprint on the base of the clip but you very seldom find prints on a gun. However, I'll process it for fingerprints as soon as we get to Headquarters."

Tragg inserted a pencil in the barrel of the gun, opened a dispatch case he was carrying, carefully fitted the gun into a metallic cradle and was about to close the lid when Burger said, "Look for the number."

Tragg again inserted the pencil in the barrel, lifted out the gun, then checked the number.

"The number," he said, "is C 48809."

Burger consulted his notebook. "All right," he said, "that's the first one he bought."

Burger regarded Mason thoughtfully. "I am going to tell you, Mason, if there's been any substitution of guns in this case I'm going to proceed against you. . . . I'll throw the book at you."

"What do you mean, substitution of guns?"

"Garvin Hastings bought two identical thirty-eight-caliber revolvers in his lifetime," Burger said. "We've looked up the records and find that one gun was purchased about two years ago, and one about fourteen months ago. When he bought the second gun he told the salesman at the sporting goods store that he wanted a weapon for his wife's protection."

"And this is the second gun?" Mason asked.

"This is the first gun."

"Then I don't see what all the shouting is about," Mason told him.

"I'll tell you what the shouting is about," Burger said. "You love to mix us up and mix guns up, and my best guess is that your client had access to both guns. You switched guns after firing a couple of shots from the wrong gun. I'll bet ten to one that when we process this gun at ballistics we'll find that it was *not* the gun that killed Hastings."

"In that event," Mason said, "you won't have a case against Adelle Hastings, will you?"

Burger said angrily, "I'm completely out of patience with you, Mason, and I'm out of patience with your tactics. We just *may* have a murder case against both Adelle Hastings and Perry Mason. If you've juggled the evidence I'm going to hold you as an accessory after the fact, and in this state the distinction between principals and accessories is abolished. In other words, I'll be holding you for murder."

"That's in the event this gun is *not* the fatal gun."

"That's right."

"But suppose it *is* the fatal gun?"

Hamilton Burger said, "Then I'll hold you for . . ."

"Yes?" Mason prompted, as Burger's voice trailed off.

"Before I go any further," Burger said, "I'm here to take an official statement from you as to why this gun wasn't available earlier in the day."

"All right, I'll tell you," Mason said. "Adelle Hastings told the story of the stolen purse and the gun to Simley Beason, who is the office manager for the Garvin Hastings Enterprises. Beason very unwisely felt that the gun might be incriminating evidence and he might help Adelle Hastings by removing that gun.

"He came to my office at six o'clock this morning, convinced a charwoman who was cleaning the office at that time that he was Perry Mason. He was carrying a brief case. He walked brazenly into the office, opened the drawer in my desk, took out the gun and took it to the offices of the Hastings Enterprises.

"He has a locker there. He wrapped the gun in tissue paper. Then wrapped it with brown paper. He typed out a label identifying the contents as being a gun that had been taken from the office of Perry Mason, put his signature on it, taped it to the paper and sealed the paper with tape."

"Why did he do all that?" Tragg asked.

"Because he wanted to protect Adelle Hastings and he was afraid that there was some possibility the claim might be made she had been the one who had taken the gun."

Tragg and Burger exchanged glances.

"Go ahead," Burger said. "You always have an almost plausible story. I'm not believing, but I'm listening."

"I knew that somebody had stolen the gun," Mason said. "I felt it had to be someone who knew where to look for the gun. I felt that probably the only time it could have been stolen was around the time the cleaning women came to the offices in the morning. I had Paul Drake look up the register of people coming to the office. I got a description of the one man who had been here. I ran down a few other clues and they pointed to Simley Beason. I asked him to come to the office, charged him with the theft and had the charwoman come in here to identify him. She identified him. He broke down and confessed."

"All right, tell us about the gun," Burger said wearily. "Something seems to tell me this is all part of the same old run-around, only now you've given it a new twist."

"So," Mason said, "Simley Beason telephoned his secretary, Rosalie Blackburn, told her to go to his desk, get the key to his locker, open the locker, take the golf clubs out of his bag, turn the golf bag upside down, take the package that was in the bottom of the golf bag and bring it up here."

"Go ahead," Burger said. "This is your show. Keep talking."

"When the secretary came here," Mason said, "she gave the package to Beason, but pointed out that the package was not sealed when she found it. The paper had been cut with a very sharp knife or perhaps a razor blade. Apparently the person doing that had unwrapped the paper, looked at the gun, then replaced the package in the bottom of the golf bag."

Burger's eyes narrowed.

"Now then," Mason said, "I'm giving you all the information that I have on the subject. As soon as I had the weapon again in my possession I put it in the desk drawer, being careful not to touch it with my hands and leave any fingerprints, and called Lieutenant Tragg."

"That's your story?" Tragg asked.

"That's it," Mason said.

Tragg again exchanged glances with Burger.

Burger's face darkened. "You can't get away with this, Perry," he said.

"I'm not getting away with anything. You wanted my story. I told it to you."

Burger said, "This is all very clever. When we try Adelle Hastings for murder and try to introduce this gun in evidence you're going to claim that we can't prove it was the same gun that was in Adelle's purse. You've told this cock-and-bull story with the idea that you'll force us to put this man, Beason, on the stand, then this secretary of his. Then you'll claim that the package was tampered with, you'll claim that anyone had a chance to substitute guns and that it can't be shown this was the gun that Adelle Hastings had in her purse."

"Well," Mason said, smiling, "what's wrong with that? If you're going to introduce this gun in evidence against Adelle Hastings, you've got to *prove* it was the gun that came from her purse."

"If you had taken the number of the gun when you first found it in the purse," Tragg said, "it would have removed any doubt."

Mason said, "Then you'd have claimed I handled the gun too much."

"I suppose you threw away the paper that had been cut so we won't have any evidence of that?" Tragg said.

"On the contrary," Mason told him, "I very carefully saved that paper, being careful not to get any new fingerprints on it."

Mason nodded to Della Street.

She went to the storage closet and returned with the cardboard carton.

"The paper," Mason said, "is in there."

"I presume," Hamilton Burger said, "you're a witness to all of this, Miss Street."

"Well, not all of it," Della said. "While Simley Beason was here, Gertie, the receptionist and switchboard operator, was out to lunch and I had to mind the switchboard. I didn't hear *all* of the conversation that took place."

"Pretty damned clever," Burger said. "This is a nice way to complicate the situation so we can't tie the murder weapon in with the defendant. It's happened before but it isn't going to happen again."

"Why isn't it going to happen again?" Mason asked.

"Because you won't be here," Burger said. "You'll be in San Quentin. I'm tired of this and I'm not going to put up with it. You're always juggling evidence around. This time you've worked this two-gun hocus-pocus so you hope that you can convince a jury that someone tampered with the evidence."

"I think someone did tamper with the evidence," Mason said. "I also think that someone deliberately attempted to frame Adelle Hastings for murder."

"Well, we'll just take the evidence and—"

"Now, wait a minute," Mason interrupted. "If you're going to take the wrapping paper out of this office you're going to examine it right here so there can be no question that the paper had been cut open and—"

"Oh, I'll concede that the paper had been cut open," Burger said wearily. "That was all part of the scheme. But I'll tell you what we're going to do with you, Perry Mason. We're going to take both of you down to the offices of the Hastings Enterprises."

"I'm willing to go with you but Della Street has—"

"I don't care what she has," Burger snapped. "She can have a string of appointments as long as her arm but both of you are going down to that office and you're going right now."

TEN

Hamilton Burger, marching into the president's office, proceeded to take charge of the Hastings business enterprises.

"I want all of the employees in here where I can talk with them," he said. "I am Hamilton Burger, the district attorney. This is Lieutenant Tragg of the homicide division of the metropolitan police, and I have with me Mr. Perry Mason, an attorney who is representing Adelle Sterling Hastings, the widow of Garvin S. Hastings. And this is his secretary, Miss Della Street.

"Now, I want to get everybody together and I want some information about things that have happened here."

There was an authoritative ring to Hamilton Burger's voice, an ability to impress people and inspire confidence, and within a few minutes the big office was crowded with employees.

"First," Hamilton Burger said, "I want to know who's in charge."

"I am," a man said.

"And who are you?"

"I'm Connely Maynard. I have for some time been directly under Garvin Hastings."

"All right, come up here by me," Burger said.

Maynard, a man in his late thirties with high cheekbones, had steady gray eyes and a firm mouth which cut in a wide straight line above his massive jaw, moved over to Hamilton Burger's side.

"What do you know about Hastings' affairs?" Burger asked him.

"I know virtually everything, Mr. Burger."

"Did Hastings have a gun?"

"He did. Actually he had two guns."

"What do you know about them?"

"They were, I believe, identical guns. Hastings purchased one gun which he kept in his house for protection. After he and his wife separated he purchased another gun. He gave her one and kept one. I don't know whether he gave her the more recent purchase or whether he gave her the one he had, and kept the more recent purchase for himself."

Burger looked at the semicircle of curious, anxious faces, said, "There's a Simley Beason here?"

Beason stepped forward.

"Now, just what's your capacity?" Burger asked.

Connely Maynard said, "Mr. Beason is directly under me. I have charge of the entire enterprises, Beason has charge of running the office."

Burger regarded Beason. "What do you know about Mr. Hastings' affairs?"

"Quite a bit," Beason said modestly, "perhaps not as much as Connely Maynard but still I know quite a bit."

"You knew about the two guns?"

"Yes."

"How well do you know Adelle Hastings?"

"I know her quite well. I think all the older employees here do, Mr. Burger. She was employed as secretary before she and Garvin Hastings were married."

"Was she popular?" Burger asked.

"I think she was."

Burger turned to Maynard. "What do you think?"

Maynard hesitated for a moment, said, "I believe Adelle Sterling, before she became Adelle Hastings, was a very competent secretary. However, since she was Mr. Hastings' personal secretary, my contact with her was confined to having her co-operate with me in the execution of instructions given by Mr. Hastings. I think that Beason, as the manager of the office, had more contact with her."

"Hastings was married when she first started working here?"

"Yes."

"To whom?"

"Minerva Hastings."

"And what became of that marriage?"

"There was a divorce."

Burger looked at Beason. "Did Adelle Hastings have anything to do with that divorce?"

Beason said, "Minerva thought so."

Burger looked around at the people in the office.

"Adelle broke up the marriage," Maynard said quietly.

"All right," Burger said, "we'll dig into this in private. Now then, what I want to know is this: Who went to Perry Mason's office at six o'clock this morning?"

"I did," Simley Beason said.

"What did you do there?"

"I took a gun out of a desk drawer."

"Why did you do that?"

"Because," Beason said with some feeling, "an attempt was being made to frame Adelle Hastings for something, and I didn't propose to stand for it."

"What's your interest in the matter?"

"I wanted to see fair play."

"What was the thing for which she was being framed?"

"I know now it was murder."

"But you didn't know then?"

"No."

"But you did know that it was something serious enough for you to be taking a chance on larceny?"

"I didn't stop to figure the legal effect of what I was doing."

"Why did you go up there at six o'clock in the morning?"

"Because I wanted to get into the office. I found out that the cleaning woman started on Mr. Mason's office at six o'clock in the morning."

"We'll go into some of this later and in private," Hamilton Burger said grimly. "What I want to know now is what you did with the gun."

"I wrapped that gun in tissue paper, then I wrapped it in heavy brown paper. I sealed the brown paper with transparent adhesive tape, then I typed a label stating what was in the package and fastened that label with adhesive tape to the paper, then I signed my name across the seals and put the sealed package in the bottom of my bag of golf clubs."

"Then what did you do?"

"I put the golf clubs in my locker, locked the door of the locker, put the key to the locker back in my desk drawer in its accustomed place. Then later on when Mr. Hastings didn't show up for his ten o'clock appointment I tried to call him, found that the tape recording answering service was still on and I drove out to Hastings' house."

"Did you get in?"

"Yes."

"How?"

"Mr. Hastings kept a key here in the office so that in case it became necessary for him to send anyone out to the house there would be a key. Sometimes he would call on long distance telephone with instructions for someone to get an article from his house, perhaps a suitcase packed with fresh clothes, perhaps some papers which he had left at the house. I've been over all this with the police, answered all their questions and—"

"Never mind what you've been over with the police," Burger snapped. "You're going over it again, all of it. You're answering *my* questions now. Where was that key kept?"

"In the closet of Mr. Hastings' private office."

"That's this office?"

"Yes."

"Show me the closet."

Beason walked over to the closet, opened the door, said, "The key hangs on this nail here."

"It's not there now," Burger said.

"No, sir," Beason said. "The police took it from me this morning."

"It was generally known where that key was kept?" Burger asked.

"I would assume so."

"All right, now what happened to that gun after you put it in the golf bag?"

"I was summoned to Mr. Mason's office."

"By whom?"

"By Perry Mason."

"And what happened there?"

"He accused me of taking the gun. I admitted it."

"Then what happened?"

"I telephoned Rosalie Blackburn, my secretary, and asked her to bring it to Mr. Mason's office."

"Which one is Rosalie Blackburn?" Burger asked.

"I am," the secretary said, stepping forward.

"All right, what did you do?"

"I got the key to the locker, took out the golf clubs, turned the golf bag upside down, took out the package and delivered it to Mr. Mason's office."

"What was the condition of the package when you first saw it?" Burger asked.

"It had been cut open with a very sharp knife."

"And what did you do about that?"

"Nothing. I could see there was a gun inside the paper. It fell out of the package to the floor when I turned the golf bag upside down."

"What did you do then?"

"I picked up the gun, wrapped it back in the paper and took the package to Mr. Beason at Mr. Mason's office."

"All right," Burger said wearily, "now I want to know who cut open that package? . . . Come on, speak up."

There was silence.

Burger said, "Very well, I'm going to tell all of you something. This is a murder case. We're not playing games here. This is a very serious matter. I want you all to understand something about the law, as well as the facts.

"Garvin Hastings was killed in his bed while he was asleep. When you kill a sleeping man it isn't manslaughter, it isn't second-degree murder. It's not done in the heat of passion, it's done as the result of cold-blooded, deliberate planning. It's first-degree murder and the penalty for first-degree murder is either death or life imprisonment.

"Any person who conceals evidence or tries to aid and abet the murderer becomes an accessory. Any person who tries to tamper with evidence is guilty of a crime.

"It is quite evident that someone has been tampering with evidence. We know that Simley Beason did. I am going to hold him strictly accountable. It also appears that after he had tampered with the evidence, some person opened that package. Now, I want to know who did it and why it was done and whether there was any substitution of weapons or any tampering with evidence.

"While you're all here some person who has significant information may not care to come forward and disclose it, but I want you to realize that you have a duty to disclose everything you know, and I feel sure that in an office this size evidence couldn't have been tampered with without someone knowing something, at least some suspicious circumstance.

"Now then, my office is going to be wide open for any incoming telephone calls and Lieutenant Tragg here, at Homicide at police headquarters, is going to be anxious to find out what happened.

"If any one of you people have any knowledge, I want you to get to a telephone sometime before the close of business this afternoon and give us that information.

"I want to impress upon you that this is a murder case and that we're not going to have any fooling around with— Who's this?"

The people near the door were thrust aside.

A thick-set individual with an aggressive manner pushed his way forward.

"I'm Huntley L. Banner, Mr. Burger," he said. "I haven't met you but I've seen you in court several times."

"And who are you?" Burger asked.

"I'm an attorney. I represented Garvin Hastings in his lifetime and I am representing his widow at the moment."

"I thought Mason was representing his widow," Burger said.

Banner said, "Mr. Mason is representing Adelle Hastings. I am representing the widow, Minerva Hastings."

"Wasn't there a divorce?"

"I think I'll let Mrs. Hastings answer that question," Banner said, and again turned toward the door.

The people nearest the door fell back, and a woman in her early thirties entered the room.

She was a striking brunette. Her chin was up, her eyes were flashing.

Banner took her arm and said, "This is Garvin Hastings' widow. This is Minerva Shelton Hastings. She owns all this business."

"Didn't you get a divorce in Nevada?" Burger asked her.

"I did not," she said. "I went to Nevada and established a residence. I filed a divorce suit. I did not carry it through to completion."

"What!" Simley Beason exclaimed.

She smiled at him triumphantly and said, "I did *not* carry it through to completion."

"But," Beason exclaimed, "you wrote Garvin Hastings that everything was taken care of, that—!"

"Certainly I did," she said. "That little strumpet in the office was trying to twist him around her finger, trying to feather her nest financially, and I decided that I would fight fire with fire."

Hamilton Burger said, "You knew that your husband was planning to marry his secretary?"

"Of course I did. That's why he virtually booted me out. I was to go to Nevada and get a divorce."

"And you filed suit for divorce?" Burger asked.

"Yes, I did," she said defiantly.

"Where?"

"In Carson City."

"Carson City?"

"That's right. I had some friends there and I felt I could accomplish what I wanted to accomplish better in Carson City than anywhere else."

"Then you wrote your husband that you had secured a divorce?"

"I did not. I wrote him that everything had been completed according to plan."

Simley Beason said, "It's all a lie. She sent him a copy of the divorce decree."

Minerva Hastings smiled at him. "I sent him what purported to be a copy of a decree," she said. "It wasn't a certified copy."

"It was a copy of a decree," Beason insisted.

"Go look up the records," she challenged, then whirled to Hamilton Burger. "Simley Beason here has always been sweet on Adelle and would love to give her a sympathetic shoulder, then marry her and step into control of the business.

"For your information, Mr. Simley Beason, I am going to be the one who controls the business. I am the widow. Adelle Hastings has no more status than any other woman."

"I think it's only fair to advise everyone," Huntley Banner said, "that I am filing a petition for the probate of a will and having Minerva Hastings appointed executrix of the estate."

"A will!" Hamilton Burger said. "He left a will?"

"That's right. It's a will leaving everything to Minerva Hastings. Garvin Hastings had no relatives."

Mason said, "Wasn't there also a later will leaving the property to Adelle Hastings after he went through a marriage ceremony with her?"

"That ceremony wasn't worth that!" Minerva said, snapping her fingers.

Mason kept his eyes on Banner. "I'm talking about a will," he said.

Banner said, "If, of course, a later will should be found, that will be another question. However, I think that you will find any later will was torn up by Garvin Hastings when Adelle and he separated. I don't care to discuss the legal points now. I am simply trying to clarify the situation so that the authorities will know exactly where we stand, and with whom to deal."

Mason said, "If your client perpetrated a fraud on Garvin Hastings, she won't be in a position to capitalize on that fraud. Having told him that she had a divorce, she will be estopped to take advantage of her chicanery."

"We'll argue the legal points in court, Mr. Mason," Banner said. "Right now I'm simply advising everyone that Minerva Hastings is going to be in control of the business and we will expect unconditional loyalty from all of the office employees."

"With the exception of Simley Beason," Minerva Hastings said acidly. "As far as you are concerned, Simley Beason, you can go and comfort Adelle as of now. Your services are discontinued. You are no longer employed here. You may clean out your desk and get your personal things out of here any time this afternoon. I will leave orders that you are not to be admitted to the premises tomorrow."

Mason said, "You can't fire him. You haven't been appointed executrix of the estate."

She turned to Connely Maynard. "You understand me, Connely?" she said. "I want Simley Beason out of here and I want him kept out. I want to see that he gets all his things out of his desk this afternoon and that he is out of the office and surrenders his key. Do you understand?"

Connely Maynard swallowed once. Then he said, "Yes, Mrs. Hastings."

"Very well," she said. "See that my orders are carried out, regardless of what any attorney tries to tell you."

With that she turned and swept imperiously out of the office, followed by Huntley Banner.

Mason said, "As far as I'm concerned, and as far as my client is concerned, orders given by Minerva Hastings are absolutely worthless. You people can do what you want to. You can take whatever action you see fit as far as your relationships are concerned, but as far as my client is concerned and as far as I am concerned, Minerva Hastings has no status. Having resorted to fraud to lead Garvin Hastings to think she had secured a divorce, she is now estopped to falsify her own utterances."

And Mason smiled at a dumbfounded Hamilton Burger, then stalked out of the office without once looking back.

ELEVEN

Back in his office Mason paced the floor, his head thrust slightly forward in frowning concentration.

After a few moments he started talking to Della Street, throwing the words over his shoulder as he paced and turned, paced and turned.

"Garvin Hastings bought two guns, Della," he said. "One of them was purchased before he married Adelle, one while he was married to her.

"Now," Mason went on, "would he have given a gun to Minerva? Remember that she had some friends in Carson City. *She* was driving back and forth—that is, we can assume she was. Hastings could have let her have his gun."

"But he gave one to Adelle," Della Street said.

"That's right," Mason said. "He gave one to Adelle. She doesn't know the number. There was no reason for her to look at the number. The way she looked at it, a gun was a gun and that was all there was to it.

"But if Garvin gave her a gun he could well have given Minerva a gun."

"That would have been the first gun he purchased," Della Street said.

"Exactly," Mason agreed.

"And it was that first gun which killed him?"

"We don't know yet. It was the first gun that Tragg took from the desk drawer.

"It would have been rather easy for Minerva to have killed him after stealing Adelle's purse, then she could have put the murder weapon in the purse, put on dark glasses, planted the purse here in this office, rushed over to Las Vegas, used a duplicate key which she had had made to Adelle's apartment, gotten in there and stolen her gun. That would leave her with Adelle's gun still in her possession."

"Unless she was smart enough to get rid of it," Della said.

"No," Mason said, "she'd be a lot smarter if she kept it. Then when someone asked her if it wasn't true that Garvin had given her a gun for her protection, she'd say, 'Why, certainly,' and produce the gun that he'd given Adelle."

"And there'd be no way of proving she was lying?" Della Street asked.

"No way on earth," Mason said. "We can *surmise* that the first gun was the one he intended to keep for himself, that the gun he bought after his marriage to Minerva was for her—a present to her for her protection.

"Give Paul Drake a ring, Della. Tell him that I want some more information on that Carson City car that was parked in the lot. It belonged to Harley C. Drexel, a contractor."

"What about him?"

"See if there isn't some connection between Minerva and Drexel. Remember that Drexel's car was parked in the parking lot down here all Monday afternoon. There were two cars with Nevada licenses. One of them was a young woman from Las Vegas and I naturally felt that she would be the one to check. But in view of later developments I'm beginning to think this Carson City car may have some significance we don't want to overlook."

Della Street put through the call to Paul Drake and gave him the instructions.

The phone rang. Della answered it, said, "Huntley Banner calling for you, Chief."

Mason picked up his telephone, said, "Hello, Mason speaking."

"This is Banner, Mr. Mason. I want to impress upon you that I had no intention whatever of representing Minerva until after the developments following Garvin Hastings' death."

"And why did you want to impress that on me?" Mason asked.

"It's a question of ethics."

"The ethics in the matter," Mason said, "are between you and your own conscience on the one hand, between you and the bar association on the other."

"I understand, but I value your good opinion."

"Don't ever try to value something you don't have," Mason said.

"Now, don't be like that, Mason. I feel that it would be a great mistake for us to get involved in litigation which would eat up the assets of the estate. After all, there are always two sides to every question, there's always a middle ground and there are enough assets here for both parties.

"I think our clients might be able to work out a settlement if we can keep personalities out of it."

"Go ahead," Mason said. "You're doing the talking."

"Well, in the first place," Banner said, "you must realize that my client has the inside track legally. Once you accept that as a fact, then we can discuss matters."

"I don't accept that as a fact," Mason said.

"I'll tell you what I'm going to do," Banner said. "I'm going to have my secretary take a copy of Garvin Hastings' will to your office."

"His *last* will?" Mason asked.

"As far as we know, it's his last will. It was made shortly after he married Minerva Hastings. He left everything to her and named her executrix of the estate."

"Then that will was invalidated by his subsequent marriage to Adelle Sterling," Mason said.

"Now wait a minute, wait a minute. That wasn't a legal marriage," Banner pointed out. "Therefore the provisions of the law regarding automatic revocation of wills in whole or in part has no application here."

"And," Mason went on, "I am inclined to think he made another will which revoked the will you're referring to."

"I don't think he did," Banner said. "If he did, I think I'd have known of it. I know what he was *intending* to do. I'll be fair with you on that.

"Actually he had given me the data and told me to draw up a will and revoke all prior wills. Then this separation with Adelle developed and he told me to hold up drawing that last will until we could negotiate a property settlement. He told me that he would give her a sum of money payable in annual installments over a ten-year period and make provision for her in a lump sum in his will. That was all to be part of the property settlement. For that reason he instructed me to hold off drawing the will."

Mason said, "So it is your contention that the will leaving everything to your client is the only valid outstanding will?"

"I feel certain that was his *last* will. Now, I want to be fair with you, Mason. I have a machine in my office which makes photographic copies of documents and I'm going to make a copy of that will, signatures and all, and have my secretary take it to your office. You read it, look at the date, the signatures of the witnesses, and then call me."

"Who executed as witnesses?" Mason asked.

"My secretary, Elvina Mitchell, and I signed as witnesses."

"The will was signed in your presence?"

"Not only signed in our presence but Mr. Hastings declared that the document was his last will and testament and asked us to execute the document as witnesses. . . . I'm going to let you question my secretary. She'll tell you the circumstances under which the will was executed.

"After you've familiarized yourself with the circumstances, we can talk. And remember this: A murderer cannot inherit from the victim."

"Adelle is not affected in any way by that provision of law," Mason said.

"You claim she isn't."

"On the other hand," Mason went on, "how about *your* client? How do you know Minerva didn't kill him? In which event, regardless of her deception, regardless of her status as the surviving widow, regardless of the will, *she* can't inherit."

"But that's absurd," Banner said. "Minerva can't be dragged into this thing in that manner."

"You think she can't," Mason said. "For your information, there's some evidence pointing directly to her."

"What evidence?"

"I don't care to discuss it at this time."

"I'm sending Elvina—Miss Mitchell—down to your office with a photostatic copy of the will," Banner said.

"When will she be here?"

"Within the next fifteen minutes."

"All right, I'll see her. Now, she's one of the subscribing witnesses?"

"Yes."

"It's all right if I talk with her?"

"Of course it's all right. That's why I'm sending her over to talk with you. I'm putting my cards on the table, Mason."

"All right," Mason said, "I'll take a look at anything you want to show me. I'm not closing the door on a compromise, but I'm not going to be stampeded into waiving any of my client's rights."

"I don't want you to," Banner said. "I'm trying to be fair with you, Mason. I have the greatest respect for your ability and I don't want to lock horns with you."

"Then draw in your own horns," Mason said. "And if you want to show me a copy of that will, get your secretary started."

Mason hung up and turned to Della Street who had been monitoring the conversation.

"Give Elvina a good once-over when she comes in, Della. I'd like to have you size her up from a woman's standpoint."

"Think she's more than a secretary?" Della Street asked.

"That I wouldn't know but want to find out," Mason said, "but she's evidently a great little business getter. Apparently she's very friendly with Maynard and through that friendship she managed to ease Banner into the picture so that with Maynard's acquiescence, and probably little resistance from Hastings, Banner started moving in a little at a time. That probably explains a good deal of the way our client feels toward Banner, and it just *may* be that Banner has been representing Minerva all along."

"Well," Della Street said, "you don't need to *tell* me to size up Elvina. I'll certainly give her a double take."

Mason said, "Now this man, Banner, is pretty much of a schemer, himself. Notice the adroit way that he's feathered his nest. He uses his secretary to get the legal business of the Hastings Enterprises, then becomes Hastings' personal lawyer and now shows up representing Minerva."

Della Street said, "Listening to that phone conversation, it seemed to me that Banner was going out of his way to convince you that he has all the trump cards."

"He certainly is," Mason said, "and he's overdoing it so much

that you feel he's vulnerable somewhere along the line and because
he doesn't want me to discover just *where* he's vulnerable, he's trying to convince me that his position is impregnable."

"Can she get away with that, Chief?"

"With what?"

"Minerva. With pretending she had a divorce, taking Hastings'
money, assuring him that she was using it to get a divorce, then
sending him word that the divorce had been granted, getting a
lump-sum settlement, sitting silently on the sidelines while he went
through what apparently was a bigamous marriage, and now showing up to claim the estate."

Mason said, "There are some interesting legal questions, Della. She
is not claiming the estate as the surviving widow alone. She's claiming it under the terms of a will which was never changed."

"Doesn't the law give any protection whatever to Adelle?"

"That," Mason said, "depends on a lot of factors; whether the
marriage to Adelle was void from the beginning, or whether it is a
ceremony that is effective until it is vacated by court decree. The
law provides generally that if a person marries after making a will,
any prior will is revoked as far as the surviving spouse is concerned.
That rule of law is of course subject to certain exceptions but that's
generally the rule."

Mason walked over to the shelf of reference books lining one
side of his office, took down Volume 53, California Jurisprudence
2d, thumbed through the pages and said, "Here's a summary of the
California law on it, Della. You might take this down:

> To have the effect provided for in the statutory pro-
> visions, the testator's post-testamentary marriage must be
> valid. But since there is a presumption that a marriage
> properly performed is valid, the party claiming the post-
> testamentary marriage of the testator to have been invalid
> has the burden of proving this contention.

Of course there may have been some recent decisions on this point
in the last two or three years since this particular volume was
printed, and we'll have to do a little research work. But I think we
can safely act on the assumption that this is the law."

The telephone rang, and Della, picking up the instrument, said, "Yes, Gertie."

Della listened for a moment, then said, "You mean his secretary is here. . . . Wait just a minute, Gertie."

She turned to Mason and said, "Huntley Banner is here himself, not his secretary but the lawyer."

Mason replaced the law book on the shelf, said, "Tell him to come in, Della."

Della hurried to open the connecting door and Banner entered the office, his face smiling, his manner conciliatory.

"I'm certainly sorry about that scene down at the Hastings offices," he said. "My client has always hated Simley Beason and she blew her top. Naturally, as her attorney, I had to back her play. You'll understand that. Of course you have to make allowances for the fact that she's been under very great strain, but even so the matter *could* have been handled much more diplomatically."

"Sit down, Banner," Mason said. "I thought your secretary was coming over."

"I did too," Banner said. "I told her to come over here but she got stage fright. She was afraid you'd start cross-examining her about the execution of the will and all of that and she chickened out on me. So I told her I'd come myself.

"After all, it's only a hop, skip and a jump. Our offices are just a block and a half apart, and I wanted to show you the photostat of the will. I've already filed the original with a petition for probate."

Mason extended his hand for the papers which Banner held out.

"You'll notice," Banner said, "it's a very short will. He simply revokes all prior wills, states that he is of sound and disposing mind and memory, that he has no living relatives other than his wife, Minerva Shelton Hastings; that he therefore leaves all his property to her.

"Then we have a safety clause in it, for whatever it's worth, providing that if any person should appear and claim relationship any sort to him, whether as descendant, common-law wife or othe wise, and establish such relationship, that person is left the sum · one hundred dollars.

"Now then, you'll notice the will is executed in the presence of witnesses and the witnesses are Elvina Mitchell and myself.

"If you'd like to ask any questions about that will, go right ahead."

"That will was executed at the date appearing in the will?"

"That's right. It was executed in my office. Garvin Hastings signed it in my presence and in the presence of Elvina Mitchell, the other witness. He asked us to sign as witnesses and declared in our presence that this was his last will and testament. That will is absolutely ironclad."

"How soon after his marriage to Minerva was the will made?" Mason asked.

"I think within forty-eight hours. As I remember it, he rang me up and told me that he was getting married, that he wanted his wife to have protection."

"What about his estate prior to that time?" Mason asked. "He must have had a will."

"I don't know about the terms of *that* will," Banner said. "I wasn't his attorney at that time."

"Then you started doing his legal work at about the date he married Minerva?" Mason asked.

"I didn't say that," Banner said. "Now, don't put words in my mouth, Mason. Actually I had been doing some legal work for him for a period of several months prior to the execution of this will, but shortly after this will was executed I began doing more and more of his work and he began to rely on me more and more. I think I was doing his legal work exclusively at the time this will was executed."

"Then his marriage with Minerva went on the rocks?" Mason asked.

"Well, it depends on what you mean by that. Actually his marriage started breaking up about . . . oh, I'd say about the time Adelle Sterling was employed as secretary.

"Now, I'm not saying anything against your client, Mason, but I will say that it was the contention of Minerva that the marriage would have continued if it hadn't been for Adelle. She claims that Adelle insinuated herself into Hastings' confidence and alienated his affections."

"So then Minerva went to Nevada to establish a residence and get a divorce?" Mason asked.

"That's right. There's no secret about that. Hastings told her that he thought the marriage was a failure and that he thought they should dissolve it. I believe it was at that time he told her that he had fallen in love with his secretary, that he wanted to be free to marry her, that he wanted Minerva to go to Nevada and get a divorce."

"And Minerva agreed?" Mason asked.

"No, she didn't," Banner said. "She filed suit for divorce right here. She named Adelle as corespondent. She asked for separate maintenance and a big chunk of alimony. She also asked that a receiver be appointed to take charge of the property. She demanded attorney's fees and all the rest of it."

"What happened to that suit?" Mason asked.

"There's no question about *that* suit," Banner said. "That suit was dismissed. I checked on that personally."

"What caused her to dismiss it?"

"Hastings went to her and persuaded her that it would be better for her to dismiss the suit and give him his freedom."

"What did he use as a persuader?" Mason asked.

"It's anybody's guess," Banner said. "Hastings didn't tell me the amount. It was a personal conversation between Hastings and Minerva and I didn't want to have anything to do with it because actually Minerva had an attorney of record."

"What happened to him?"

"I suppose Minerva compensated him in some way—that is, Hastings did. Anyway, it was all taken care of very hush-hush and Minerva got a check for, I believe, some two hundred or two hundred and fifty thousand dollars and went to Nevada, established a residence, and agreed to get a divorce.

"Now of course you heard her state that she decided to fight fire with fire, that she told her husband she had secured a divorce and sent him what purported to be a copy of the decree of divorce, but that decree wasn't certified.

"Now that of course is fraud, and whether she can capitalize on that fraud is a legal question, but there were very great pressures being brought to bear upon her and she did what she thought was best to protect her interests.

"The fact remains that legally she still remained Hastings' wife and Hastings' marriage to Adelle was therefore bigamous and void."

"No property settlement was ever executed between Minerva and Hastings?" Mason asked.

"Not to my knowledge. Hastings simply went to her apartment and said, 'Look here, Minerva, why do you want to get an attorney and fight this thing through the courts? When you get done the lawyer will get a big percentage of what you recover, and you *may* not get a dime. Virtually all the property is my sole and separate property and'— Well, he intimated that he'd had detectives on her trail and that there was some scandal in connection with her."

"You don't know what it was?"

"No, I don't."

"Don't you know, or aren't you saying?"

"Honestly, Mr. Mason, I don't know. Hastings never confided in me on that point and of course Minerva hasn't. It was a private conversation and I don't know what happened. I do know generally that there was something in Minerva's past that Hastings had found out about, something that she didn't want to have publicized— Well, I guess it was a standoff and they made this settlement."

"But no papers were ever drawn?"

"No papers were ever drawn. She agreed to dismiss the action down here, to go to Nevada and get a divorce and stipulate in the divorce decree that there had been a complete property settlement made and she waived all claims to alimony."

"And she deliberately planned to double-cross him all the time she was making that settlement," Mason said.

Banner shook his head. "I don't think so, Mason, I think she intended to live up to the terms of the agreement. I think it was made in good faith, but afterwards when she saw the manner in which Adelle was insinuating herself into Hastings' life— Well, of course you can't understand the emotions of women; they do strange things.

"I'm not here to state that my client is completely blameless, but I am here to state that, in my opinion, her legal position is impregnable and I'm here to make a reasonable settlement."

"I take it you've checked the records to find that there was no final decree of divorce in Nevada?" Mason asked.

"That's right, Mason. I've checked the records on that point. Naturally I did that before I agreed to represent Minerva.

"She filed the action, all right. She stayed there for six weeks, established a legal residence, filed the action—and then just never did bring the action to trial."

"But she did send a forged decree of divorce to her husband."

"No," Banner said.

"Now wait a minute," Mason said, "she admitted as much in the presence of witnesses there at the company offices."

"No, she didn't," Banner said. "There's a peculiar distinction, Mason. That decree of divorce wasn't forged."

"What do you mean?"

"She was smart enough not to sign the name of any judge to what purported to be a copy of the decree. She simply signed a purely fictitious name. It may be a fraud. I doubt if it is a forgery. There's no question but what she was guilty of fraud. As between her and Hastings, if Hastings had lived, there would have been an action for fraud. But as between her and her husband's mistress, the situation is different.

"My client isn't blameless but, on the other hand, she's still the wife of Hastings. That is, she's his widow."

The phone gave several short, sharp rings—Gertie's signal of an emergency.

The door from the outer office opened and Lt. Tragg entered the room.

"Well, well, Perry," he said. "I seem to have caught you busy. Hello, Banner, what are you two doing? Hatching up a plot of some kind?"

Mason said, "Tragg never does me the courtesy of having the receptionist announce him. He always walks right in this way."

"That's right," Tragg said, beaming. "The taxpayers don't like to have us cooling our heels in some attorney's office and if you know I'm coming you have a chance to prepare yourself a bit in advance."

"How much preparation do you think I need?" Mason asked.

"Not very much," Tragg said. "I came to advise you, Perry, that I'm here to pick up your client."

"On what charge?"

"Murder, of course," Tragg said cheerfully. "That gun turned out to be the fatal gun, and we found a fingerprint on it."

"You don't get fingerprints from guns," Mason said. "You, yourself admitted that, Tragg. Moreover the gun was handled by Beason and by his secretary after . . ."

Tragg was positively beaming. "This isn't a fingerprint powder would bring out, Perry," he interrupted, "it's very unusual. Quite a break, I'd say."

"Fingerprint of my client?" Mason asked.

"I don't know yet," Tragg said. "We haven't taken her prints. We're going to. I'm pretty sure, however, it's the print of a woman and—that's quite a break, you know, Perry. I don't believe there's one time out of twenty-five that we can get a fingerprint off a gun —I'll make it one in fifty—and, as I said, this isn't the usual type of fingerprint. The person who handled it had evidently been eating candy, or handling a type of nail polish or some liquid cement. While the print is dry and powder won't stick to it, it's nevertheless visible, and a very workable print."

"What if I don't surrender my client?" Mason asked.

"Then we'll get her," Tragg said, "and of course we'll have a point in our favor because we'll let it be known that we had told her not to leave town, that we'd get in touch with her through you if we wanted her. And now we've told you we want her."

Tragg settled himself comfortably in a chair, smiled at Banner and said, "How are you doing, Banner?"

"Very well," Banner said, grinning. "Very well indeed!"

Mason nodded to Della Street. "You win, Tragg," he said. "Get Adelle Hastings on the phone, Della, and tell her to come at once."

TWELVE

Judge Quincy L. Fallon looked down over the crowded courtroom and said, "This is the time heretofore fixed for the preliminary hearing in the case of the People of the State of California versus Adelle Sterling Hastings. Are you ready?"

Morton Ellis, one of the trial deputies of the district attorney's office, said, "Ready for the People, Your Honor."

Mason stood up. "If the Court please, the defendant is ready."

"Very well," Judge Fallon said. "Now, I want to make a few comments before we start taking evidence in this case.

"The Court understands from the press that a legal battle is going to be waged for the control of the estate. Minerva Shelton Hastings claims under a will, and Adelle Sterling Hastings, the defendant in this case, claims as the surviving spouse. Both parties have filed petitions which will duly be heard in the probate court.

"Now, this Court doesn't intend to have this hearing in the criminal case develop into a squabble as to who is entitled to the estate or the management thereof. The sole question to be determined here is whether a crime has been committed and, if so, whether there is reasonable ground to believe the defendant is guilty of that crime. If she is, she will be bound over for trial in the superior court, and if she isn't, she will be released.

"The Court realizes that it may be necessary to show *some* of the facts connected with the claims to the estate for the purpose of showing motivation, and quite possibly bias of the witnesses. But the Court wants the evidence concerning control of the estate limited

123

to that purpose. It will serve no particular purpose to try the probate matter here, or for counsel to go on a fishing expedition with the different witnesses in the hope that some statement will be made which can be used in the probate hearing.

"With that in mind I caution you, gentlemen, to limit your examination, and in particular your cross-examination, within the bounds delineated by the Court.

"You may proceed, gentlemen."

Morton Ellis, with crisp, businesslike efficiency, hurried through the opening stages of the trial.

A surveyor introduced a diagram of the premises, a floor plan of the upper and lower floors of the Hastings mansion. There were photographs of the exterior of the mansion. An autopsy surgeon testified that death was caused by two bullets from a .38-caliber revolver which had penetrated the brain; that the body had been found in bed; that death was instantaneous; that the man had evidently been killed while he was asleep; that the time of death had been sometime early in the morning of Monday, the fourth; that death could have been as late as eight o'clock in the morning of that day, or as early as one o'clock in the morning; that in his opinion the body had not been moved after death but had been found in exactly the position in which it had been lying when the shots were fired; the post-mortem lividity indicated as much.

Ellis said, "I will call Lieutenant Arthur Tragg as my next witness."

Tragg came forward, was sworn, took the witness stand and told of the discovery of the body and introduced photographs of the body lying in the bed, the room in which the body had been found; and then produced the fatal bullets, one of which had been removed from the mattress after having passed entirely through the head; the other had been found inside the skull.

"Are you acquainted with Perry Mason, the attorney for the defendant?" Ellis asked.

"I am."

"Have you had occasion to talk with him over the telephone from time to time?"

"I have."

"Are you familiar with the sound of his voice?"

"I am."

"I will ask you whether or not you had any conversation with Perry Mason on the morning of Tuesday, the fifth?"

"I did. Yes, sir."

"And what was that conversation?"

"Mr. Mason called me, he told me that someone had been in his o fice the day prior to the telephone call."

"Now, just a minute," Ellis said, "that would have been Monday, the fourth."

"That's right."

"And what else did Mr. Mason say?"

"He said that this caller had left a woman's handbag in the office, that the handbag contained a gun, that the gun had been fired twice. He said further that subsequently the bag had been identified as being the property of Adelle Sterling Hastings, the defendant in this case, and suggested that I might care to examine the weapon."

"And what did you do?"

"I asked one of the men on the homicide squad to put through a call to Garvin S. Hastings and get him on the phone. However, shortly after that a report came in that one of Hastings' employees had gone to the house to see why Hastings had not been answering the phone and had found the man's body in bed."

"So what did you do?"

"I went to Mr. Mason's office."

"And what did you find there?"

"I found the defendant there."

"Did you find the gun Mr. Mason had referred to?"

"Not then."

"Did you subsequently locate it?"

"Just a moment," Mason said. "I object to that question as calling for a conclusion of the witness."

"Why, he certainly can answer whether or not he eventually discovered the gun," Ellis said.

"No, he can't," Mason said, "because he has no way of knowing whether the gun he discovered was the same gun that I had referred to over the telephone, or the same gun that I had in my office."

"Oh, Your Honor," Ellis said, "this is simply quibbling. We can trace that gun from the woman's handbag to Mason's desk, from Mason's desk to the office of Garvin Hastings, where one of the employees, Simley Beason, had concealed it, and then we can trace it into the possession of Lieutenant Tragg."

"Then go ahead and trace it," Mason said, "but don't ask this witness if the gun that he eventually recovered was the same gun that was in my office drawer. That's a conclusion."

"All right, all right," Ellis conceded with poor grace. "I'll withdraw the question and I'll ask the witness this question: Did you inquire about the gun when you went to Mr. Mason's office?"

"I did."

"Did you ask him to produce it?"

"I did."

"And what, if anything, did Mr. Mason do in connection with that request?"

"He opened a drawer in the right-hand side of his desk and seemed very much surprised when he found that the drawer was empty."

Morton Ellis said, "I will ask you, Lieutenant Tragg, if you have certified copies of the firearms record in your possession showing the sales of firearms to Garvin S. Hastings."

"I have."

"Will you please give me those records?"

Tragg passed over two sheets of paper.

"What do these records show generally, Lieutenant?"

"Those are official documents which are kept in accordance with the provisions of California law. They show the purchase of two guns from The Sportsman Supply Center."

"And what do these documents cover, Lieutenant?"

"The purchase of two weapons, two Smith and Wesson thirty-eight-caliber revolvers of similar model. The first one is for a Smith and Wesson gun with a two-and-a-half-inch barrel, number C 48809, which was sold on the date appearing on this sheet. The other was purchased some months later and is for a similar model Smith and Wesson gun, with the serial number C 232721."

"Very well. Now will you tell us what conversations you had with Perry Mason, as attorney for the defendant, in connection with this firearm which he told you about and which he said he was unable to produce after you had reached his office."

"Mr. Mason told me that he had taken a gun from the defendant's handbag which had been left in his office; that he had placed that gun in the upper right-hand drawer of his desk; that the gun had disappeared."

"Now, when did this conversation take place, Lieutenant?"

"This was on Tuesday, the fifth."

"And did Mr. Mason tell you what he had done with reference to trying to locate that gun?"

"He did, at a later conversation."

"What did he say?"

"He said that he had made an investigation himself and through his private detective, Paul Drake, head of the Drake Detective Agency; that as a result of that investigation he found that a man had entered his office on the morning of Tuesday, the fifth, at about the time the charwoman was cleaning up the office; that this man had been carrying a brief case and had represented himself to be Perry Mason—if not in direct words, at least by his conduct— and had gone on into the office, stayed there for about ten minutes and then had left.

"Mr. Mason told me that by a process of reasoning and detective work he had located this man and learned his identity, that the man was Simley Beason, the office manager of the Hastings Enterprises."

"Did he tell you anything else?"

"He said that Simley Beason had taken that gun and had wrapped it up in paper and then sealed the paper, and had deposited the package in the bottom of a golf bag."

"And then what?"

"He said that Mr. Beason in his presence had telephoned his secretary—Beason's secretary—to take the gun from the golf bag and bring it to Mason's office; that when the secretary arrived it appeared the wrappings had been tampered with."

"And did Mr. Mason say what he did with reference to that gun?"

"He called me on the telephone and told me that he had the gun for me and later on told me that he also had the wrappings in a box which I could look over for fingerprints if I so desired."

"And what did you do?"

"I went to Mr. Mason's office and picked up the gun."

"Did you subsequently make ballistics tests with that gun?"

"I did."

"And did you try to match up the specimen bullets which you

fired from that gun with the fatal bullets, one of which had been taken from the body of Garvin Hastings, and one of which had been taken from the mattress?"

"I did."

"What did you find out?"

"The fatal bullets were fired from this weapon."

"I show you a weapon, being a Smith and Wesson revolver, number C 48809, and ask you if you recognize this weapon."

"I do, yes, sir. It has my mark on it and I have a note of the number."

"Is that the gun that you received from Mr. Mason?"

"It is."

"Lieutenant, did you examine this gun for fingerprints?"

"I did."

"Did you find any fingerprints on it?"

"At the time I first examined the gun I didn't find any fingerprints on it. I dusted the gun with fingerprint powder for the purpose of developing latent fingerprints. Nothing was developed that would be of help. Later on, however, when I got the gun at headquarters I found that there was a dried fingerprint on the weapon. This fingerprint did not take powder because there was no moisture left in it. It was a print which had thoroughly dried. It had been handled by some person whose finger contained some sticky substance, such perhaps as sweetened saliva, or perhaps which had come from moist tobacco. Anyway the fingerprint could be observed in a certain light."

"Did you photograph that fingerprint?"

"Yes, sir."

"You have that photograph here?"

"Yes, sir."

"Now, have you checked that fingerprint to find whose finger made that print?"

"Yes, sir."

"Whose print?"

"That print was the middle finger of the right hand of the defendant, Adelle Hastings."

"I would like to have this revolver introduced in evidence, if the Court please, as prosecution's Exhibit B-12."

"Just a moment," Mason said. "Before I either stipulate the gun

may be received in evidence or object to it, I would like the privi-
lege of asking questions on *voir dire*."

"Very well," Judge Fallon ruled. "You may interrogate the witness."

"Lieutenant, you have stated that I told you I had *the* gun. Now,
isn't it a fact that what I told you was that I had *a* gun?"

"I think you said you had recovered *the* gun."

"That had been taken from my desk drawer?"

"That was my understanding."

"Did I tell you that the gun came from the defendant's handbag?"

"Now wait a minute," Tragg said. "Actually, I believe the conversation about the gun was with you, and then it appeared the gun
had disappeared and then I believe your secretary called me and
told me that the gun which had been misplaced had now been
found and was available."

"Now, I told you, did I not," Mason asked, "that Simley Beason
had taken this gun from my office and wrapped it in paper, sealed
the paper, but that when the package was returned to my office the
paper had been cut with a razor or sharp knife and there was no
way of telling that this was the gun which had come from the defendant's handbag?"

"Objected to as calling for hearsay evidence," Ellis said.

Mason said, "That's not hearsay evidence. Lieutenant Tragg has
testified as to what I told him. I am now trying to test his recollection
by cross-examining him on the entire conversation."

"The objection is overruled. Answer the question," Judge Fallon
ruled.

"Yes," Tragg said.

"So," Mason said, "if what I told you is correct, there is no way
of showing that this gun is the one that I took from the defendant's
handbag or the one that Simley Beason took from my office."

"Objected to as being argumentative and calling for a conclusion
of the witness," Ellis said.

"Sustained," Judge Fallon said.

Mason smiled. "Lieutenant Tragg," he said, "you have identified
this gun as the gun from which the fatal bullets were fired?"

"Yes, sir."

"You know therefore it is the gun with which the murder was
committed."

"Yes, sir."

"You have never seen that gun in the possession of the defendant, have you?"

"I have not. No, sir."

"Exactly. And from what I told you in the conversation you have testified to, you can't swear that after Simley Beason took this particular gun, wrapped it and put it in the golf bag, someone didn't take out the package, slit the paper, unwrap the gun, wrap up another gun in the paper and put it back in the bottom of the golf bag, can you?"

"The same objection," Ellis said.

"If the Court please," Mason said, "this is a different question. I am asking him now if *as a result of the conversation he had with me,* he can connect that gun with the defendant."

"The objection is overruled," Judge Fallon said. "I think this question is legitimate cross-examination in regard to the conversation that the witness had with Perry Mason."

"No, sir," Lt. Tragg said, *"from what you told me* I can't positively swear that this gun hadn't been substituted after Simley Beason took it. I can't positively swear that the gun that you gave me was the gun that you took from the woman's handbag, and I can't positively swear *from your conversation* that this identical gun was connected with the defendant; that is, you understand, Mr. Mason, *from your conversation,* from what you told me.

"I can, however, swear from a fingerprint that this gun had been handled by the defendant at a time when she had some foreign, sticky substance on the middle finger of her right hand."

"Exactly," Mason said. "That substance could have had sugar in it?"

"Yes, sir, sugar, nail polish, mending cement, any one of a dozen things."

"And had dried?"

"Yes, sir."

"And left a latent print to which dusting powder did not adhere?"

"Yes, sir."

"And yet it was a lasting latent print?"

"Yes, sir."

"The average latent print, containing moisture and sebaceous matter retains its moisture for only a relatively short period of time?"

"Yes, sir."

"But this was a different type of print?"

"Yes, sir."

"Not as perishable as the ordinary print?"

"That's right."

"Then, for all you know it may have been left there last Christmas when the defendant was eating Christmas candy and the gun was in the possession of her husband?"

Tragg's face flushed. "I can't tell *when* the print was made."

"It *could* have been made last Christmas?"

"It *could* have been."

"Exactly," Mason said. "That is all of my questions on *voir dire*. I now object to the introduction of the evidence on the ground that it is incompetent, irrelevant and immaterial and no proper foundation has been laid."

Judge Fallon said, "The proper foundation has been laid to identify this as the murder weapon and it may be received in evidence as the murder weapon."

Ellis said, "I will now withdraw Lieutenant Tragg and call Simley Beason as a witness."

Beason marched to the witness stand as one who faces an inescapable ordeal. He raised his right hand, took the oath and after giving his name and address to the clerk, looked with steady hostility at Morton Ellis.

"Your name is Simley Beason, you were on the fourth and fifth of this month employed as office manager at Hastings Enterprises, and had been so employed for a period of some four years prior to that date?"

"Yes, sir."

"Your Honor," Ellis said, "this is a hostile witness and I am going to have to use leading questions to interrogate him."

"He hasn't shown any evidence of hostility so far," Judge Fallon said. "Proceed with your examination along the regular lines. If it becomes apparent that he is hostile I will so rule and permit you to ask leading questions."

"Very well, Your Honor."

"I call your attention to Tuesday, the fifth of the month, and ask you if you saw the defendant at that time?"

"I did, yes, sir."

"When did you first see her?"

"Somewhat early in the morning."

"How early?"

"I didn't look at my watch."

"Was it before daylight?"

"I can't remember."

"Where did you meet her?"

"At a restaurant."

"How did you happen to meet her there?"

"She had told me she would be there."

"This was an all-night restaurant?"

"Yes."

"You met with the defendant and had breakfast there with her?"

"Yes."

"And conversed during breakfast?"

"Naturally we didn't simply sit there and stare at each other."

"Just answer the questions," Ellis said. "Did you or did you not converse with the defendant?"

"I've answered the question. I told you I did."

"And following that conversation, you went to Mr. Mason's office, that is, to the building where Mr. Mason has his offices?"

"Yes."

"And entered that building?"

"Yes."

"Did you sign a register in the elevator?"

"Yes."

"Did you sign your own name?"

"No."

"You signed an assumed name?"

"Yes."

"And did you take the elevator to the floor on which Mr. Mason has his offices?"

"Yes."

"And went down to Mr. Mason's offices?"

"Yes."

"What did you do when you arrived at Mr. Mason's offices?"

"I went in."

"Was there anyone there to let you in?"

"Yes."

"Who was it?"

"A charwoman."

"And you had some conversation with her?"

"Yes."

"What did you tell her?"

"I can't remember."

"And did you take something from Mr. Mason's office?"

"I refuse to answer."

"On what ground?"

"On the ground that the answer may incriminate me."

Ellis looked at Judge Fallon.

"Very well," Judge Fallon said. "This witness is a hostile witness. You may have your ruling and use leading questions—although you have been doing so without objection from the defense. Proceed."

"Did you take a gun from Mr. Mason's office?"

"I refuse to answer on the ground that the answer might incriminate me."

"Later on in Mr. Mason's office and in the presence of Mr. Mason, did you telephone your secretary at the Hastings Enterprises?"

"Yes."

"What is the name of this secretary?"

"Rosalie Blackburn."

"What did you tell her over the telephone?"

"I told her to go to my locker, after getting a key from my desk, to take my golf clubs out of my golf bag, to turn it upside down and she would find a package wrapped in paper in the golf bag, that she was to bring me that package."

"To Mr. Mason's office?"

"Yes."

"And she did this?"

"I don't know."

"What do you mean, you don't know?"

"I don't know whether she did what I had told her to or not."

"You do know that she appeared at Mason's office with a package, do you not?"

"Yes."

"That was the same package which you had put in the golf bag?"

"I don't know."

"Well, it contained the same article you had put in there, didn't it?"

"I don't know."

"What do you mean, you don't know?"

"I took no means of identifying the article which was in there."

"That article was a gun, wasn't it?"

"The package I put in there contained a gun, yes."

"And that was the same gun you had taken from Mr. Mason's office, wasn't it?"

"I refuse to answer on the ground that the answer might incriminate me."

"But you admit you put a package in your golf bag?"

"Yes."

"And that package contained a gun."

"Yes."

"And that package was taken out of the golf bag by your secretary?"

"Objected to," Mason said, "as calling for a conclusion of the witness."

"Sustained."

"But you did *instruct* your secretary to take the package from the golf bag."

"Yes."

"And bring it to Mr. Mason's office."

"Yes."

"And she did so?"

"I don't know."

"Weren't you there? Didn't she deliver the package to you?"

"She delivered *a* package to me, but I have no way of knowing whether it was the same package that I put in the golf bag. I will add by way of explanation that I had taken steps to identify the contents of that package by carefully sealing the paper and affixing a label to the outside identifying the contents of the package. When the package was delivered to me the seals had been cut, the package had been opened, and I have no way of knowing whether the contents of the package had been substituted."

"The article that you put in the package was a gun, was it not?"

"Yes, sir."

"A thirty-eight-caliber Smith and Wesson revolver?"

"Yes, sir."

"And that was the same gun you got from Mr. Mason's office?"

"I refuse to answer on the ground that to do so may incriminate me."

"All right. Now, we'll go back to your meeting with the defendant. Isn't it a fact that your trip to Mr. Mason's office was inspired by something the defendant had told you?"

The witness hesitated.

"Well," Ellis pressed, "isn't that a fact? Go on, answer the question."

"I refuse to answer on the ground that to do so may incriminate me."

"Now, if the Court please," Ellis said, "it is quite apparent that the witness is attempting to hide behind his constitutional rights and is availing himself of them when there is no legal reason for him to do so. It may be perfectly proper for him to refuse to commit himself in connection with burglary of Mr. Mason's office, but as far as his conversation with the defendant is concerned, it was not a privileged conversation and there was certainly nothing that would incriminate him in relating that conversation."

"May I be heard?" Mason asked.

"Certainly," Judge Fallon said.

"If it should appear," Mason said, "that the defendant and this witness conspired to get some evidence from my office, then the taking of the gun would be an overt act which would make him guilty of a separate crime, the crime of criminal conspiracy. Taking the gun is one thing, conspiring to take it is another. They are both crimes."

"That's splitting hairs," Ellis said.

"No, it isn't," Mason said. "Whenever you people draw up an information or a complaint against a person you put in just as many counts as you can think of. You put in a count of criminal conspiracy and you put in a count of the criminal act. Then you try to talk a jury into returning a verdict of guilty on every count in the indictment. You claim each count is a separate crime, that you don't make the law, you only enforce it, that if the legislature has chosen to make it a crime to conspire to commit an unlawful act and a defendant conspires to commit such an act and then does commit the act, he's guilty of two separate crimes.

"Now, you can't eat your cake and have it too."

Judge Fallon twisted his lips in the ghost of a smile.

"I think the point is well taken," he ruled. "I fail to see that the conversation is pertinent or relevant unless it had to do with some aspect of this crime, and if it does it may well be that the defendant and the witness did conspire to do certain things and the witness has grounds to feel that answering the question would tend to involve him in a crime of conspiracy."

"All right," Ellis said, savagely turning to the witness, "you wrapped a gun in paper and put it in the golf bag, didn't you?"

"Yes, sir."

"Had you ever seen that gun before?"

"Before what?"

"Before you put it in the golf bag."

"Yes, sir."

"Where?"

"I refuse to answer on the ground that the question may incriminate me."

"Had you ever seen it prior to the fifth of this month?"

"I don't know."

"Why don't you know?"

"Because I don't know whether this was the same gun I saw or not."

"You saw a gun that was like it in appearance?"

"Yes."

"Where?"

"I can't recall all the places I have seen similar guns. The company undoubtedly manufactures hundreds of thousands of these guns and I have seen them in display cases in sporting goods stores, and in various other places."

"And," Ellis said, leveling an accusing forefinger at the witness, "some of those 'other places' included a woman's handbag, did it not?"

"Yes."

"What woman?"

The witness hung his head. "Mrs. Hastings," he said.

"Aha!" Ellis said. "Now, after all this painful agony of examination you admit that you saw this gun in the handbag of the defendant."

"Now, just a moment, if the Court please," Mason said. "I object to the side comments by counsel and also to the question itself. The witness didn't say he had seen *this* gun in the defendant's handbag."

Morton Ellis said, "It could have been the same gun, for all *he* knows."

"And it could have been a different gun, for all *you* know," Mason said.

"I'm going to sustain the objection to the question in its present form," Judge Fallon said.

"Very well," Morton Ellis said, "we'll let it go at that. Now then, was any statement made to you as to where the gun came from?"

"Yes, sir."

"What was the statement?"

"Mrs. Hastings said that her husband had given it to her and told her to keep it in her handbag, that he believed in women having some form of protection when they were out alone at night. If she should have a blow-out or car trouble of some sort she would be completely helpless stalled by the side of the road."

"That," Morton Ellis announced triumphantly, "is all."

"Just a moment," Mason said. "I have a question or two on cross-examination. You have said that you saw such a gun in the handbag of Mrs. Hastings?"

"Yes, sir."

"And that Mrs. Hastings told you her husband had given it to her for her protection, particularly when she was driving at night?"

"Yes, sir."

"Did she say anything about how often she carried it?"

"Well, not in so many words, but I gathered that she carried it a good deal of the time in her handbag."

Judge Fallon looked at Ellis. "That of course is a conclusion. Does the prosecution wish to strike it out?"

Ellis smiled and said, "The prosecution does not wish to strike it out, Your Honor. Let defense counsel go right ahead. Such a cross-examination may be a little hard on his client but the prosecution certainly doesn't want to stop it in any way."

"There is no need for making such a comment," Judge Fallon

said. "The Court merely called attention of the prosecution to the fact that the witness had testified to an obvious conclusion."

"And the prosecution has no desire whatever to interpose objections to this line of testimony," Ellis said.

Mason turned to the witness. "You gathered from the conversation you had that she had been given this gun, that it was her property?"

"Yes, sir."

"And that she was carrying it?"

"Yes, sir."

"And knew how to use it?"

"Yes, sir."

Ellis turned to survey the spectators in the courtroom with a broad, triumphant grin.

"And you say this was Mrs. Hastings, with whom you had these conversations?"

"Yes, sir."

Mason's eyes twinkled. "Was it Adelle Sterling Hastings, the defendant in this action?"

"No, sir. Those conversations were with Minerva Shelton Hastings, the former wife."

Abruptly the grin faded from Ellis's face. A look of sickly consternation replaced it as he jumped to his feet. "Now just a moment, Your Honor, just a moment," he said. "This now appears to have been a carefully planned trap hatched up between defense counsel and this witness, knowing that when he said Mrs. Hastings I would assume he meant the defendant. I object to these questions, I move to strike out the answers on the ground that they are conclusions of the witness."

Judge Fallon said sharply, "You had your opportunity to interpose an objection. The Court noticed the manner in which the witness referred, not to the defendant, but to Mrs. Hastings, and knowing that there were two Mrs. Hastings the Court followed the examination with considerable care. The witness carefully refrained from ever mentioning the defendant. He referred simply to Mrs. Hastings."

"It was a trap—a deliberately prepared trap," Ellis said.

"I know of no law," Judge Fallon said, "which prevents defense counsel from putting traps along the road he expects his adversary to follow. I'm afraid, Mr. Deputy District Attorney, you're going to have to look out for your own traps. In view of the fact that there were two Mrs. Hastings, the Court noticed the peculiar wording of the answer of the witness and wondered if you intended to ask the witness to specify which Mrs. Hastings he was referring to. The answers will stand.

"Do you have any more questions of this witness, Mr. Mason?"

"I have no further cross-examination," Mason said.

Beason started to leave the stand.

"Just a moment, just a moment," Ellis said. "I have a couple of questions."

Beason settled back into the seat.

"You discussed your testimony with Mr. Mason before coming into court?" Ellis asked.

"Yes, sir."

"And did Mr. Mason tell you that you probably would be asked if you had ever seen a gun similar in appearance to the one which has been introduced in evidence in this case as the murder weapon?"

"Yes, sir."

"And did you tell Mr. Mason that you had seen such a gun in the possession of Minerva Hastings?"

"Yes."

"And didn't Mr. Mason tell you that if you had an opportunity you were to state that you had seen such a gun in the possession of Mrs. Hastings, without mentioning that it was Minerva Hastings?"

"He said something to that effect, yes."

"Now then," Ellis said, smiling triumphantly, "did you ever see a similar gun in the possession of the defendant, Adelle Sterling Hastings? Now, answer that question yes or no."

"Yes."

"Was it in her handbag?"

"Yes."

Again Ellis turned to the spectators in the courtroom with a triumphant smile. "That," he announced, "is all."

Again Beason started to leave the stand.

"Just a moment," Mason said, "I have a few questions on recross-examination.

"Did you ever see a gun in her purse more than once?" Mason asked.

"Yes. There was another time."

"When was that?"

"I can't remember the exact date."

Mason said, "Then you saw *two* guns in her possession. One," Mason said, holding up the index finger of his left hand, "the gun that the decedent purchased which was not the fatal gun, and two," here Mason held up the index finger of his other hand, "the gun that *was* the fatal gun?"

"Just a minute, just a minute," Ellis said, "I object to the question as calling for a conclusion of the witness."

"I don't see how that calls for a conclusion of the witness," Mason said.

"He can't tell whether there were two separate guns," Ellis said. "Unless he compared them with the numbers he doesn't know what gun it was."

Mason smiled at Judge Fallon. "I think," he said, "the district attorney has made my point perfectly. The witness saw a gun. He doesn't know whether it was the fatal gun which some murderer had substituted in the witness's golf bag, or whether it was a weapon which the decedent had given the defendant for her own protection and which had been stolen from her."

Mason made a little bow to the assistant district attorney and said, "And, if the Court please, that concludes my recross-examination."

"Now, wait a minute," Ellis said, "that's not a fair presentation. The witness should answer the question."

"He can't answer the question," Mason said, "because you've objected to it."

"Well, there hasn't been any ruling of the Court," Ellis said, and then added suddenly, "I'll withdraw the objection."

"Very well," Mason said, "answer the question, Mr. Beason."

"I don't know what gun it was," Beason said. "It could have been the same gun both times, it could have been different guns, it could have been any gun. I understand that Smith and Wesson manufactures thousands of guns, all of which are identical."

Ellis said irritably, "It's quite easy for the witness to answer the question in that manner after counsel has so adroitly pointed out the proper answer to make under the guise of making an objection."

"If the Court please," Mason said, "I didn't make the objection. The prosecution did that."

"I have no further redirect," Ellis said.

"That's all, Mr. Beason. You're excused."

"You're excused," Judge Fallon said to the witness.

Ellis glanced at the clock.

Judge Fallon nodded imperceptibly, said, "It is the hour for the usual noon adjournment. Court will recess until two o'clock this afternoon."

The spectators rose as Judge Fallon left the bench and went through the door leading to his chambers.

Mason caught Simley Beason's eye and beckoned to him.

Taking Beason's arm, Mason stood close to him where there was no chance of being overheard and said, "What were you afraid of, Beason?"

"Afraid?" Beason asked, his voice showing surprise. "What do you mean, afraid? I wasn't afraid. I didn't want to help the prosecution's case any more than necessary."

Mason said, "You were afraid, Beason. There was too much relief in your manner when the deputy district attorney said he had no questions on redirect."

Beason shook his head, his expression one of puzzled innocence. "Why no, Mr. Mason, you have me wrong."

Mason said, "I don't think I've made any mistake, Beason. I've examined too many witnesses in court and seen too many people under the stress of emotion to make that much of a mistake. What information were you withholding that you were afraid the prosecution was going to inquire about?"

"Absolutely nothing," Beason said.

"All right," Mason told him, "we'll let it go at that."

Beason caught Adelle Hastings' eye as a policewoman took her arm to escort her to the jail. Between them flashed a look of significant understanding, a momentary glance of triumph.

THIRTEEN

A French restaurant some three blocks from the courthouse traditionally held a small intimate private dining room for the luncheon use of Perry Mason, Della Street and Paul Drake, and in the past many conferences held in this dining room during lunch hours had resulted in last-minute changes in strategy.

Now seated around the circular table with a telephone plugged in so they could receive and send out calls, Drake said, "I've picked up a tip, Perry. They have a surprise they're springing this afternoon."

"Any idea what it is?"

"No."

Mason said, "There's something Simley Beason was holding back. I don't know what it was. He was afraid they were going to ask him some particular question, and the answer to that question might well have been devastating as far as the defendant was concerned.

"When they let him off the stand without asking that question his face showed relief."

"Any idea what it could be?" Drake asked.

"It might be anything," Mason said. "Of course the prosecution knows he's a hostile witness and they're afraid to ask him general questions because he might have an answer that would crucify them. However, we're probably out of the woods now. I doubt very much if they'll recall him. It's a certainty that I'm not going to call him as my witness and let them tear into him on cross-examination.

"What have you found out about the Carson City angle, Paul?"

Drake took out his pocket notebook. "There's something here that baffles me. This Harley C. Drexel, the contractor, lives at 291 Center Street, Carson City. He's a guy fifty-five years old, with a good reputation. He has a house that he built himself on a deep lot with a little bungalow in back of the house that he rents out. He's a widower, he has a daughter who's attending college somewhere in the east—supposed to be nice people."

"Any connection whatever with Adelle Hastings or anybody else who has any connection with the case?" Mason asked.

"Now, there's a funny thing," Drake said. "I ran on this by accident. I told you that Drexel rents out the building in the back of his place from time to time. It's a small compact bungalow cottage. Remember, Perry, his address is 291 Center Street. Now, when Minerva filed divorce proceedings in Nevada, the divorce proceedings she didn't ever follow up, the address she gave was 291½ Center Street. So evidently Minerva established a residence in Drexel's house, and presumably got quite well acquainted with him. Then, when we have this mysterious purse business in your office, Drexel's car is parked in the parking lot half a block from your office."

Mason's eyes widened in surprise, then narrowed in thoughtful concentration.

"What do you know about Drexel?" he asked, after a moment. "A ladies' man?"

"A contractor," Drake said, "who is concentrating on his contracting. He plunges right into the job alongside his workmen and puts in a day's work himself from time to time. Mostly he's a building contractor and carpenter; a plain, unimaginative horny-handed sort of chap."

Mason digested this information.

The waiter came and took their orders.

Abruptly Mason got up and began pacing the floor.

"It has me stumped," Drake said. "It means something, but what?"

Mason said nothing, but continued pacing the floor.

Abruptly the lawyer paused, turned to Drake, said, "Paul, here's something else. Rosalie Blackburn, Simley Beason's secretary, went to Carson City and got a divorce. Find out if she also lived at 291½ Center Street while she was establishing her residence. If she did, it will indicate a pattern of some sort that we should follow up.

"Now here's something else. I want to find out about charter planes that went to Las Vegas on the afternoon of Monday, the fourth. When Della Street and I flew in that evening, our pilot told us a representative of the Chamber of Commerce was checking charter flights. Get your men on the job, check with the Las Vegas Chamber of Commerce. Find out if this checking was on the up and up, and if it was, find out what other charter flights came in that same night *earlier* in the evening.

"I'm going up to court as soon as we finish eating, Paul, and you can get busy on the telephone."

Drake put through the call to his office and gave the necessary instructions.

"What else do you want, Perry," the detective asked, holding the phone, "anything?"

Mason, who had resumed pacing the floor, said, "What's the name of Harley Drexel's daughter?"

Drake looked at his notebook. "Helen."

"She goes to college in the east?"

"Yes."

"And is home for the summers."

"That's right."

"What's the date Minerva filed her action for divorce?" Mason asked.

"September fifteenth," Drake said promptly.

"All right," Mason said, "it takes six weeks to establish a residence in Nevada, so that means Minerva was in the Drexel house during the summer months. If Helen was home for her vacation there's a darn good chance the two women got to know each other. The Drexel car was in the parking lot all Monday afternoon. Find out where Helen is now."

Again Drake passed instructions over the wire.

"Anything else, Perry?"

"Not at the moment," Mason said.

Drake said into the phone, "Get busy on those angles right away and report as soon as you've found out anything."

The detective hung up the phone.

Mason, pacing the floor, said, "Damn it, Paul, there are a lot of angles to this case. If a lawyer is really going to represent a client he has to do a terrific amount of investigative work, and the more he does the more he has to do."

"I'll say," Drake agreed. "How are your chances on this case, Perry?"

"Right at the present time," Mason said, "we don't stand a whisper of a chance of getting Adelle Hastings off at this preliminary hearing. We stand a chance of beating the case when we try it before a jury in the superior court, because there's no way on earth the prosecution can prove someone didn't tamper with the evidence, and there's all the circumstantial evidence in the world to prove that they did.

"The prosecution can't prove the case against Adelle Hastings beyond all reasonable doubt unless they can show that it was the murder weapon that was in her purse. So far we know there were two guns in the case; one gun that Garvin Hastings bought some time ago, the other one a gun that he bought shortly after his marriage to Adelle.

"Now, there's every inference that the gun that we'll refer to as the Adelle gun, which was the last one bought, was the one that he gave her; and we know that the gun we'll refer to as the Garvin gun was the fatal gun."

"You're overlooking the fact that the fatal gun has the defendant's fingerprint on it," Drake said.

"No, I'm not," Mason said. "Remember, the defendant was married to Garvin Hastings and lived in the house with him for some time. Garvin Hastings had that gun. Probably he kept it under the pillow at night. The defendant could have been using nail polish or polish remover, and touched her middle finger to that gun. She could have been eating candy and left a fingerprint. The very nature of that fingerprint is that it is a permanent fixture as far as the gun is concerned. In other words, it could have been made any time."

Drake said, "That's a pretty theory, Perry, but you aren't going to be able to prove it."

"I don't have to prove it," Mason said. "All I have to do is raise a reasonable doubt in the minds of one of the twelve jurors."

Drake said, somewhat skeptically, "You're probably the one man on earth who could do it."

The waiter brought their food. Mason ceased pacing the floor long enough to seat himself at the table and eat sparingly of the light lunch he had ordered.

Suddenly the lawyer snapped his fingers. "I think I've got it, Paul," he said.

"Got what?" Drake asked.

"The answer we're looking for. Get your office on the line. Tell them to go to the Las Vegas airport and check the persons who rented drive-yourself cars."

"But what are you looking for?" Drake asked. "What do you expect to find?"

"I'm toying with a theory, Paul. I may be able to convince a jury that my theory is sound."

"You think you can show them what actually happened?"

Mason said, "I can show them what *could* have happened, and the prosecution can't prove it *didn't* happen."

FOURTEEN

By two o'clock Judge Fallon's courtroom was crowded.

Paul Drake whispered to Perry Mason, "Here's Hamilton Burger coming in to sit in on the case this afternoon. You know what that means. It means they've got some sort of a surprise they're going to throw at you."

Mason merely nodded.

A policewoman brought Adelle Hastings into court.

Mason turned to her, said in a low whisper, "Adelle, there's one thing in this case that bothers me."

"Only one?" she asked.

"Well," Mason said, smiling, "one main point. When Simley Beason was on the witness stand he was dreading some question the district attorney was going to ask."

"Poor Simley," she said, "he wants to protect me and yet he knows the authorities would just love to arrest him for perjury or as an accomplice or something."

"All right," Mason said, "you left the Hastings residence about what time on Monday morning?"

"It was early. I guess it was perhaps six o'clock."

"And where were you during the day?"

"I'm afraid that I am going to have to hold out on you on that point, Mr. Mason. I know a person shouldn't hold out on his attorney."

"I'll ask you one question," Mason said, looking her directly in the eye. "Were you with Simley Beason?"

Her eyes faltered. "I . . ."

A bailiff said, "Everybody stand."

The spectators and attorneys got to their feet.

Judge Fallon entered from chambers, stood for a moment at the bench, then seated himself and nodded.

"Be seated," he said.

Judge Fallon frowned thoughtfully. "I notice that the district attorney is present in court and sitting at the counsel table. Is it your intention to participate in the prosecution of this case, Mr. District Attorney, or are you here in connection with another matter?"

"I wish to appear in connection with this case," Hamilton Burger said.

"Very well, the record will so show," Judge Fallon said. "You may proceed with your case, Mr. Ellis."

Ellis engaged in a brief whispered conference with Hamilton Burger, then said, "If the Court please, while I had announced that I had completed my examination of Mr. Beason, I now find that there are two or three more questions I would like to ask. I therefore ask the Court's permission to recall him for redirect examination."

"Permission is granted," Judge Fallon said. "Return to the stand, Mr. Beason. Remember you're already under oath."

Beason got up, started up the aisle, hesitated briefly, then squaring his shoulders marched through the swinging gate in the bar and up to the witness stand.

Hamilton Burger rose to face the wintess.

"Directing your attention to Tuesday morning, the fifth of this month, did you and the defendant have breakfast together?"

"Yes."

"Directing your attention to Monday, the fourth of this month, did you and the defendant also have breakfast on that morning?"

"Now, if the Court please," Mason said, "this is apparently merely an attempt to smear the defendant. The defendant had been a faithful wife but had been asked to leave the place which she had made into a home and told to go to Las Vegas and get a divorce, that her husband no longer loved her. She followed those instructions to the letter and certainly anything that was done in connection with meeting other men or talking with them, or having meals with them, is entirely justified. The sole purpose of this testimony is to discredit the defendant in the public press."

"We're going to connect it up," Hamilton Burger said.

"The objection is overruled," Judge Fallon said. "I will state that I probably would have sustained the objection if the question had related to any other meal than breakfast, but a breakfast is certainly not the result of a casual meeting. Proceed."

Burger turned to the witness. "Answer the question," he said.

"Yes," Beason said.

"Mr. Beason, were you in the office where you are employed all the day on Monday, the fourth of this month?"

"No, sir."

"Where were you?"

"Objected to as incompetent, irrelevant and immaterial," Mason said.

Judge Fallon hesitated a moment, then said, "I'm going to sustain the objection at this time. I think the prosecution is trying to connect up all of this, but one piece of extraneous evidence cannot be used to connect up another piece of evidence which is equally extraneous."

"If the Court please," Hamilton Burger said, "if we could have just a little leeway here we could connect this all up."

Judge Fallon said, "The expression, a little leeway, Mr. Prosecutor, indicates that you want to get just a little bit off course and the Court has a duty here to protect the rights of the defendant. I am going to sustain the objection."

"Were you in company with the defendant on Monday, the fourth?" Hamilton Burger asked.

"Objected to, if the Court please; incompetent, irrelevant and immaterial," Mason said.

"I'm going to overrule that objection. The witness will answer the question."

Beason looked at the defendant, then hastily averted his eyes.

"Yes," he said at length. And then added, "During part of the time."

Hamilton Burger said, "All right, since it seems impossible to connect this up except by asking leading questions, I will ask you this: Isn't it a fact that on Sunday, the third, you and the defendant drove to Ventura where you inspected a piece of property that the defendant was thinking of buying and on which she wanted your opinion?"

"Now, you can answer that question yes or no."

Beason again shifted his position, then said, "Yes."

"And at that time didn't the defendant state to you in the presence of a real estate broker that the price of the property was more than she could afford to pay, that she couldn't raise that much actual cash?"

"Yes."

"Then, on the following day, on Monday, the fourth, didn't the defendant ask you to meet her for breakfast at an early hour in the morning? Didn't she tell you at that time that things were going to work out so she could make the cash payment on the Ventura property and that she was going up and close the deal?"

"Well . . . Yes."

"And did the defendant tell you what had happened between Sunday night, the third, and early Monday morning, the fourth, which had changed her condition so that she could close a deal on the property?

"Didn't she tell you Garvin Hastings was dead and that she expected to be wealthy?"

"No. She said she had made a settlement with him that would enable her to go ahead with the purchase."

"And didn't the defendant meet you on the morning of Tuesday, the fifth, at an early breakfast before six o'clock and ask you to take the gun from Mr. Mason's office?"

"No."

"You did have breakfast with her on the morning of Tuesday, the fifth?"

"Yes. I want to explain my answer, however, by stating that it is always my custom to eat breakfast at five-thirty in the morning at a certain restaurant. I am an early riser and the defendant knew that."

"How did she know it?"

"I have told her from time to time."

"You had discussed your eating habits and your sleeping habits with the defendant?"

"I had told her that I usually ate breakfast around five-thirty in the morning."

"That's all," Hamilton Burger said, and sat down with a triumphant smile.

"No further questions on cross-examination," Mason said.

The discomfited Simley Beason left the witness stand.

Hamilton Burger, who had now taken active charge of the case, said, "I want to call Huntley L. Banner to the stand."

Banner came forward and was sworn.

"Your name is Huntley L. Banner, you are an attorney at law duly licensed to practice in this state?" Hamilton Burger asked.

"Yes, sir."

"And during his lifetime, you were the attorney for Garvin S. Hastings?"

"During the latter part of his life, yes."

"Did you prepare a will for Garvin Hastings?"

"I did."

"That will was executed?"

"It was."

"Did you prepare another will for Hastings?"

"I did."

"Was that will executed?"

"No."

"Directing your attention to the executed will," Hamilton Burger said, "I show you this copy of a will purporting to be signed by Garvin S. Hastings, as testator, and by yourself and one Elvina Mitchell as witnesses, and under the terms of which will all the property is left to Minerva Shelton Hastings. Is that the will you refer to as the executed will?"

"It is."

"Will you please tell the Court the circumstances under which that will was executed?"

"Mr. Hastings came to my office. He had previously instructed me to prepare such a will. I had the will prepared, I handed it to him, he read it, he executed it in the presence of Elvina Mitchell and myself, he stated that it was his last will and testament, he asked us to subscribe our names as witnesses and we subscribed our names as witnesses in the presence of Garvin Hastings and in the presence of each other."

"Now, what about this other will that was not signed?" Hamilton Burger asked.

"Garvin Hastings intended to make another will, leaving the bulk of his property to the defendant, Adelle Hastings, but differences developed before such a will was executed.

"I may state that I drew up two or three tentative wills, that there was some question as to exactly what property Garvin Hastings wanted to leave her. He wanted to leave some property to trusted employees in his business, men who had been with him for years.

"While this mattter was being held in abeyance Garvin Hastings decided that his marriage was not working out the way he had anticipated. He suggested that his wife, the defendant in this case, go to Las Vegas, establish a residence and get a divorce. It was, as far as I know, a very friendly and amicable separation.

"However, it was necessary to negotiate a property settlement in connection with such divorce action and an arrangement was made by which Hastings was going to pay her a sum of money over a period of ten years and leave her a further sum in his will. Because those sums were the subject of negotiation, Hastings asked me to postpone drawing the will in final form."

"And that was the status of the matter at the time of his murder?" Hamilton Burger asked.

"Yes."

Hamilton Burger said, "This will is a certified copy. Where is the original?"

"The original is on file in the probate department. Minerva Shelton Hastings, the executrix in that will, is seeking to have the will admitted to probate and I am representing her as her attorney."

Hamilton Burger said, "I offer this certified copy in evidence, if the Court please."

"Do you have any objection, Mr. Mason?" Judge Fallon asked.

"I don't know, Your Honor. I want to cross-examine this witness on the *voir dire* before stipulating that the will may be admitted."

"Very well, cross-examine."

"Elvina Mitchell is your secretary?" Mason asked Banner.

"Yes, sir."

"She is in court?"

"No, she is not."

"She isn't?" Mason asked in some surprise. "She is a subscribing witness to the will. Do you understand that she is not to testify?"

"There has been no request for her to appear and testify. No subpoena has been served on her."

"In that event," Mason said, "and as part of my examination on the *voir dire,* I want to have a subpoena issued for Elvina Mitchell. I want her to testify."

"Surely," Hamilton Burger said, "this will, in view of the testimony of this witness, is certainly authenticated sufficiently to enable me to offer it in evidence. If counsel wishes to object on the ground that it is incompetent, irrelevant and immaterial, that is one thing. But as far as the authenticity of the document is concerned, it has been established.

"This court has stated the probate issues are not to be tried here. I have shown this will to be properly authenticated."

Mason said, "On *voir dire* I am entitled to take this document by its four corners and examine it. It is, if the Court please, an unusual document. It is a will made in favor of a wife who assured the testator she had secured a divorce from him."

"That's not in evidence," Hamilton Burger said, "and the will was executed before there was any talk of divorce."

"I'm going to put it in evidence," Mason said, "before I permit this will to be introduced."

Judge Fallon looked down at Hamilton Burger. "This is a peculiar situation," he said. "Apparently we have a will made prior to the marriage of the testator to the defendant, leaving all the estate to a former wife who presumably was divorced. Can you explain that, Mr. Burger?"

"I think it can be explained," Hamilton Burger said. "The woman was not divorced at that time. She has never been divorced. But I don't think we have to go into it at this time."

"Well," Judge Fallon said, "if the document is to be introduced in evidence in this case, and the defendant wants to bring out facts in connection with that document before it is introduced, I certainly am disposed to let the defense go ahead.

"The Court will take a thirty-minute recess and that will enable the defense to have ample opportunity to subpoena Elvina Mitchell for the defendant's *voir dire.* Court will take a thirty-minute recess."

"My secretary can't leave the office at this time," Banner said. "I have some very important matters there and we can't leave the office unattended."

"You've completed your testimony," Judge Fallon said. "You can go back and sit in the office. This matter pending before this Court is quite important, and there's certainly something sufficiently pe-

culiar about the execution of such a will so that this Court is going
to give the defense every opportunity on *voir dire* to inquire into
the circumstances."

"He can only inquire into the execution of the will, if the Court
please, not into the circumstances surrounding it."

"We'll argue that point when we come to it," Judge Fallon said.
"Court is going to take a recess for thirty minutes and defendant
will have an opportunity to serve a subpoena on Elvina Mitchell and
have her here. If she is not here at that time, Court will take a further
recess until she *is* here."

Judge Fallon got up and left the bench.

Banner hurried down to have a whispered conference with
Hamilton Burger.

Mason turned to Della Street, said, "Della, I have a hunch."

"What is it?" she asked.

"Telephone the office," Mason said. "Tell Gertie to grab a cab and
come up here. Now, when Gertie comes I want her seated, not with
the spectators, but over to the right in the jury box. I want her to
have one of the office stenographers with her. Just the two of them
seated there in the jury box."

"Will Judge Fallon permit it?" Della asked.

"Judge Fallon will permit it," Mason said. "I'll ask him for permission in chambers."

Paul Drake pushed his way forward and said, "Perry, is there any
reason why Adelle Hastings would have taken an airplane late Monday afternoon and flown to Las Vegas?"

Mason frowned and said, "I don't know, Paul. I had assumed from
what she had told me that she had taken her car and driven to Las
Vegas. But apparently she didn't start until after she had gone to
Ventura to close the deal on this piece of property on which she
was negotiating with the advice and assistance of Simley Beason.

"That property was probably one of the big things on her mind.
It was for that reason she was carrying a large sum of cash in her
purse. She wanted to make a down-payment which would bind the
deal. Why do you ask, Paul?"

Drake said, "I found out one of the things the prosecution has in
reserve. That survey by the Chamber of Commerce in Las Vegas
was on the up-and-up. They were making a survey to find out how
many charter planes came in, in the course of a single evening; how

many passengers they brought in, and just how important the charter service was."

"Go ahead," Mason said.

Drake said, "They have a witness under subpoena, a charter pilot
named Arthur Cole Caldwell. He has a flying service and he left
Los Angeles at five-thirty Monday night with a woman who had
telephoned in a reservation for a charter plane. She wanted to fly to
Las Vegas and wanted the plane to be ready to get into the air the
minute she got there. She had telephoned at two o'clock in the
afternoon and asked particularly to have this plane ready."

"If she was in such a hurry," Mason asked, "why didn't she leave
earlier?"

"The prosecution's theory," Drake said, "is that Adelle was in
your office and then went to see Simley Beason and arranged with
him to steal the gun out of the handbag she had inadvertently left
in your office; that she didn't have time to drive back to Las Vegas
and then return to Los Angeles, so she chartered a plane."

"Will Caldwell identify her?" Mason asked.

"Apparently he will; although the woman who chartered the
plane was wearing dark glasses at the time, and he admits he didn't
get too good a look at her. However, he did charter a plane to
someone who grabbed a taxi at the Las Vegas airport, went to Las
Vegas, was in Las Vegas about an hour, then returned to the plane
and was flown back to Los Angeles."

Mason's eyes narrowed thoughtfully. "Della Street and I took a
plane only a little after that, Paul. We had a twin-motored plane."

"This was a twin-motored plane."

"We couldn't have been too far behind," Mason said.

"Just long enough for your client to get in, have a drink, undress
and take a bath," Drake said.

Mason said, "It had been my idea that someone flew in to get
Adelle's gun so it could have been substituted for the murder
weapon and—"

"Exactly," Drake interrupted. "That's the prosecution's theory.
Only they think that Adelle killed Hastings with his own gun, that
she then intended to fly to Las Vegas, get *her* gun, substitute it for
the fatal gun in her handbag and throw the fatal gun away where it
would never be found.

"However, they think she was in such a hurry to put this

through at split-second timing that she inadvertently left her hand-bag in your office and you uncovered the gun which was the *real* murder weapon. That meant her only hope was to get the gun out of her apartment, have Simley Beason get to your office early in the morning and make a substitution."

Mason thoughtfully digested the information, said, "How did Caldwell make the identification?"

"From a photograph," Drake said. "They put dark glasses on a photograph and Caldwell said it looked like the person he had flown to Las Vegas. They also let him peek into the detaining room and get a peek at her. You know how the police handle these things, Perry."

"What else have you found out, Paul?" Mason asked.

"That address in Carson City," Drake said. "Helen Drexel, Har-ley Drexel's daughter, is a friend of Connely Maynard. Her father had built a little house on the back of his lot. It was not the type of house that would readily rent to permanent residents, but it was an ideal place for persons who were coming to establish a six weeks' residence in order to be able to file suit for divorce.

"So Maynard quite naturally took it up with his girl friend, Elvina Mitchell, and she arranged to tout for the place and keep it filled up."

Mason's eyes narrowed. "Then, if Minerva Hastings went there to establish a residence in order to get her divorce, Minerva must have been friendly with Banner at that time."

"Or, with Banner's secretary," Drake said.

"Then Banner was representing Minerva all along and was re-sponsible for the situation getting to a point where Hastings thought he was divorced, made a bigamous marriage and still had a legal wife in the background."

Drake nodded and said, "The friendship is between Helen Drexel and Elvina Mitchell. On the Monday in question, Helen Drexel had driven the family car in to do some shopping in Los Angeles. Since she always runs in to have a visit and a coffee break with Elvina Mitchell when she's in town, and since the parking lot next to the building here was as centrally located as any, with reference to the shopping district on the one hand and Banner's office on the other, she parked her car there and left it there while she did her shopping. It doesn't have anything to do with the murder case but it's an interesting fact, just the same, and it shows some sort of a tie-in."

"I'll say it does," Mason said. "Thanks for the information, Paul. I'm going to think it over and see if I can't make something out of it."

FIFTEEN

As Judge Fallon ascended the bench after the thirty-minute recess, Hamilton Burger said, "If the Court please; the prosecution intends to call a witness who will identify the defendant as being a person whom he saw at a certain place. At the time, the defendant was wearing dark glasses.

"In order to be fair to both the witness and the defendant, it is imperative that at the time this witness sees the defendant for the first time in court he sees her wearing dark glasses. I am going to ask the Court to instruct the defendant to put on dark glasses during this session of the court, and to keep them on."

Judge Fallon shook his head. "I doubt that that is a fair request," he said. "Personal identification is a field in which we have far too many mistakes as it is. If we force a party to put on dark glasses it would only be a step to asking that a holdup suspect put on a mask so the witnesses could identify him."

"If the Court please," Hamilton Burger said, "many things go toward making an identification; voice, manner, the shape of the head, the manner in which a person walks. I feel that the request is reasonable."

Judge Fallon started to shake his head, then caught Mason's eye.

Mason said, "We are perfectly willing to have the defendant put on dark glasses, if the Court please, provided *all* the witnesses are required to put on dark glasses and wear them at the same time that the identification is made."

Burger's face lit up triumphantly. "You're willing to do that?"

"We're willing to do that."

"That seems most reasonable," Burger said.

Judge Fallon still seemed dubious. "I think counsel is putting his client in a dangerous position. The Court has seen enough of eye-witness identification of strangers to realize the fallibility of that testimony, at best. Props of this sort can make it at its worst."

"We're perfectly willing," Mason said, with a wave of his hand. "Let them *all* put on dark glasses."

"Very well," Judge Fallon said. "All witnesses who are in court, if you have dark glasses you may put them on. If you don't have dark glasses you may leave the courtroom temporarily.

"Call your witness, Mr. Burger."

Mason turned to the defendant. "Put on your dark glasses, Adelle," he said.

Hamilton Burger settled back in his seat with a smile.

One of the officers whispered to him and Burger said, "If the Court please, Miss Mitchell has been delayed for just a few minutes. In order to save time, I would like to put on another witness out of order."

"We have no objection," Mason said, "with the understanding, however, that as soon as Elvina Mitchell enters the courtroom she will be called as a witness and this witness the district attorney is calling out of order may step down."

"That is perfectly agreeable," Hamilton Burger said. "I call Arthur Cole Caldwell."

Caldwell, a well-built, slender-waisted individual of thirty-five or thirty-six, took the witness stand.

"Your name is Arthur Cole Caldwell, you are an aviator and have an airplane charter service here in Los Angeles?"

"Yes, sir."

"Did you on Monday, the fourth, have occasion to charter an airplane to a young woman for a trip to Las Vegas?"

"Yes, I flew her to Las Vegas and then flew her back."

"How long was she in Las Vegas in all?"

"A little over an hour."

"What time did you leave?"

"We left the airport here at five-thirty. The charter had been arranged over the telephone earlier in the day and my plane was all gassed up and waiting to take off."

"Was there anything peculiar about the appearance of this person who chartered the plane?"

"Yes, sir."

"What was it?"

"Despite the fact that it was dark for a large part of the trip, she insisted upon wearing dark glasses *at all times* when she was in the plane."

Burger said, "I'm going to ask you to look around the courtroom and see if you can see that same person who chartered your plane."

"Now, if the Court please," Mason said, getting to his feet, "we object to this *means* of identification. An identification should be made in a lineup where there are several persons similar in appearance."

Judge Fallon said, "That of course is a better way to make an identification. However, that goes to the weight of the evidence, not to its admissibility. I think a question of this sort is perfectly permissible. If the prosecution wishes to make its identificaton in this manner, I overrule the objection."

The door of the courtroom opened and Elvina Mitchell hurried into the courtroom.

"If the Court please," Mason said, "Elvina Mitchell has now entered the courtroom and I request permission to put *her* on the stand immediately in accordance with the stipulation of counsel."

"Very well," Hamilton Burger said. "I will abide by my stipulation."

Burger waited until Elvina Mitchell had been sworn and seated herself on the stand. Then he said, "Your name is Elvina Mitchell and you are employed as secretary for Huntley L. Banner, an attorney in this city?"

"Yes, sir."

"How long have you been so employed?"

"For some seven years."

Burger, carrying the photostatic copy of the will, approached the witness.

"I show you a photostatic copy of a document which purports to be a last will and testament executed by Garvin Hastings and signed by you and Mr. Banner as witnesses. Are you familiar with that document, and is that your signature?"

"Yes, sir. It is."

"Were you all three present when that document was signed?"

"Yes, sir."

"And you signed as a witness?"

"Yes, sir."

"Cross-examine," Burger snapped.

Mason said, "I have here a pair of dark glasses. Would you kindly put them on?"

She stiffened. "Why should I?"

"Because," Mason said, "as you will notice, the witnesses are wearing dark glasses and that is in accordance with a stipulation made with the prosecution that any witness could be called on to put on dark glasses."

"Well, I'm certainly not a party to any stipulation. I'm not going to put on dark glasses."

"Come, come," Judge Fallon said, "I don't see the reason for this— or that is, I didn't see the reason for it at the time the stipulation was made, but this is an unusual situation. I can't see where there would be any harm resulting to this witness from putting on dark glasses."

Hamilton Burger said, "Oh, I'm quite satisfied the witness is perfectly willing to put on dark glasses. It is very apparent that Mason is trying to confuse the witness who has just left the stand, but—"

"I don't think we need to have any comments, Mr. Prosecutor," Judge Fallon said. "The witness will please put on the dark glasses."

The witness defiantly put on the dark glasses, turned her head to glare at Judge Fallon.

"That's fine," Mason said, "now will you please face me?"

She turned and faced him.

"Are you sure this is the will you witnessed?" Mason asked.

"Yes."

"Do you object to wearing those dark glasses while you are being interrogated?" Mason asked.

"I object to being *ordered* to wear them," she flared. "I am not a dog to be ordered around."

"Then you may take them off and hand them to my receptionist," Mason said, turning his back on the witness and walking back to the counsel table.

Elvina Mitchell snatched off the glasses, unhesitatingly took the two steps necessary to reach the jury box, handed the glasses to

Gertie then hurried toward the rear of the courtroom, where she stood for a few moments just inside the door.

"Mr. Caldwell will return to the stand," Hamilton Burger said.

The aviator returned to the stand.

"Now, if the Court please, Mr. Mason has interposed an objection to my question and the objection had been overruled, so I now—"

"Oh, I'll withdraw the objection," Mason said. "It's very obvious what the district attorney has in mind. I don't think it's a fair method of making an identification but let the witness answer."

Caldwell said, as one who chooses his words with great care, "The person sitting at the bar beside Mr. Perry Mason, the defendant in the case, has a very striking resemblance to the person who chartered that airplane."

"You may cross-examine," Hamilton Burger said.

"But is she the *same* one?" Mason asked. "Can you *swear* on your oath that this person is the one who chartered the plane, or was it the person whom you previously saw on the witness stand?"

The witness rubbed the angle of his jaw thoughtfully and said, "I can't be *absolutely* positive."

Mason said, "Oh, just a minute. There is one more question I *would* like to ask Miss Mitchell. Will the bailiff try and get her and bring her back, please? She can't have gone very far."

Judge Fallon looked at Mason thoughtfully, said, "Mr. Bailiff, will you try and return Miss Mitchell to the stand?"

The bailiff hurried from the courtroom.

Mason engaged in a whispered conference with Adelle Hastings, then turned to the witness.

"Your passenger wore dark glasses all the time?"

"Yes, sir."

"Both going and coming?"

"Yes, sir, all the time."

"You couldn't see her eyes at all?"

"No, sir."

"Did you see the young woman who is Mr. Banner's secretary on the stand a few moments ago?"

"Yes, sir."

"Saw her with dark glasses?"

"Yes, sir."

"Did she look like your passenger?"

The witness hesitated, then said, "Actually when I saw her I realized how hard it is to identify a woman who is wearing dark glasses. She *did* look a lot like my passenger. I now believe any young woman of similar build, wearing dark glasses, would be hard to identify.

"I also noticed Miss Mitchell's voice was a great deal like . . . Could I hear the defendant speak? That might help me make up my mind."

"So your own mind isn't made up now?"

The witness hesitated, then said, "My mind was almost made up. I had previously been given an opportunity to identify the defendant when she was not wearing dark glasses. I had said that if I could see her with dark glasses I thought I could make a positive identification.

"When I saw her with dark glasses, I felt certain but then I saw this Miss Mitchell with dark glasses and, above all, when she spoke and I heard her voice . . . Well, she sounded exactly like the person whom I flew to Las Vegas. . . . I am not completely certain."

The bailiff pushed open the swinging door and said, "I can't get her, Your Honor. She saw me coming, started to run and dashed down the stairs and mingled with a crowd in the assessor's office. I lost her."

"You *lost* her?" Judge Fallon asked. "Couldn't you pick her out of a crowd?"

"I could recognize her all right but I couldn't catch her. She was running as fast as she could go. She's younger than I am," the bailiff said. "I tried to get people to stop her but she went right on through."

"I think," Judge Fallon said, "we will adjourn court until tomorrow morning at ten o'clock. In the meantime I would like very much to get at the bottom of all this.

"I would like to have opposing counsel meet with me in chambers, immediately after court adjourns."

SIXTEEN

Judge Fallon took off his robe, hung it up on a hanger in the closet, turned to Hamilton Burger and said, "What's your explanation of all this, Mr. Burger?"

Burger, coldly indignant, said, "It is simply another razzle-dazzle. The witness, Elvina Mitchell, was suffering from stage fright and didn't want to appear in a crowded courtroom. Mr. Mason capitalized on that to terrify her into flight and now he's going to use that to try and build up favorable publicity for his client."

The judge turned to Mason. "You have a theory you're working on?" he asked.

"I have a theory," Mason said.

"Well, sit down, both of you," Judge Fallon said. "Now, Mason, let's have your theory."

Mason said, "Garvin Hastings was killed in his sleep."

Judge Fallon nodded.

Mason said, "I will act on the assumption that my client is inno- cent."

"An assumption in which I no wise join," Hamilton Burger said.

"Go ahead," Judge Fallon said to Mason.

"If my client was innocent, Garvin Hastings couldn't have been killed at night or she would have heard the shots. He must have been killed after she left in the morning to keep her breakfast ap- pointment with Simley Beason.

"That means that death took place probably between six and eight in the morning.

164

"The woman's handbag with the fatal gun in it was left in my office during the noon hour. The person who chartered an airplane to fly to Las Vegas chartered the plane by telephone and took off from the airport at five-thirty Monday afternoon.

"Banner closes his office at four-thirty. Many of the law offices close at that time.

"Therefore we have three periods of activity. Before an office opened in the morning, during the lunch hour, and after an office closed in the afternoon. That would indicate activity by a person who was employed in an office somewhere and didn't dare be absent.

"There were two guns. Garvin Hastings had one. Adelle Hastings had the other. Adelle Hastings had never looked at the number on her gun, but it is only natural to suppose that Garvin gave the new one to Adelle. The murder was committed with the older gun and that gun was in Adelle's purse. That means that someone had to get to her apartment and dispose of her gun before the authorities got there and searched the place.

"Adelle's purse was stolen after she got to Los Angeles, had driven to Ventura and then, on her way to keep her appointment with her husband, had gone in to buy cigarettes. It must have been stolen by someone who knew of her habit of wearing dark glasses, and who wanted to get the keys to her apartment."

"But why didn't that person fly to Las Vegas that Sunday night, use the keys to get into her apartment and take Adelle's gun then?" Judge Fallon asked.

"Because," Mason said, "that person wasn't sure the murder was going to be perpetrated as planned. That person couldn't be sure that Adelle Hastings was going to get up and go out to keep a breakfast appointment with Simley Beason. That person *thought* she was going to do it, but couldn't be absolutely certain.

"That person stole Adelle Hastings' bag, had duplicates made from the keys that were in that bag on Sunday evening, and waited until Adelle left the house early in the morning, leaving Garvin Hastings still asleep. Then the person slipped in quietly and carefully and deliberately made absolutely certain that Garvin Hastings was dead by pulling the trigger twice and sending two bullets crashing into the head of the sleeping man.

"Then that person put the fatal gun in Adelle Hastings' purse and planned to leave the purse in my office under such circumstances that the receptionist would swear Adelle Hastings was the one who had brought the purse to the office."

"Then why didn't that person do it before noon?" Judge Fallon asked.

"Because it was a physical impossibility for that person to do it before noon," Mason said. "That's one of the key clues in the entire case."

"Just why is that a key clue?" Judge Fallon asked.

Mason said, "Let's look at the murderer's requirements. It had to be someone who knew the business, it had to be someone who knew the habits of the household, and it had to be someone who had a job."

"You mean because of the three crucial time periods you've mentioned?" Judge Fallon asked.

"That's right," Mason said.

"Oh, Your Honor," Hamilton Burger said. "That's just another one of these razzle-dazzle run-arounds."

Judge Fallon said, "Just a moment, Mr. Burger. I'll listen to your side of the case in a few moments, but I'm very much interested in this. I'd like to hear Mr. Mason's theory."

Mason said, "Because of the manner in which the bag was left in my office the accomplice had to be a woman, although the *murderer* could have been a man.

"That narrowed the accomplice down to one of three people: Elvina Mitchell, Banner's secretary; Minerva Hastings, or Rosalie Blackburn, Beason's secretary.

"Now, I will confess that I considered each one of these persons in turn and was leaning toward Rosalie Blackburn, but then Huntley Banner told me he would send some papers over to my office by his secretary. She refused to make the trip. I wondered why at the time, but am frank to confess I didn't attach the proper importance to it.

"Then when Banner himself got on the stand to prove the will instead of having his secretary there, I began to wonder. Was it because his secretary was afraid to have Gertie, my receptionist, see her?"

"So I had Gertie seated in the jury box and another young woman with her. Then when Elvina Mitchell was rather excited and off her guard, I asked her to hand the dark glasses to my receptionist, turned my back and walked away.

"Miss Mitchell handed the dark glasses to Gertie. The point is *how did she know who my receptionist was if she hadn't been in my office?*"

"All right," Judge Fallon said, "assuming that Elvina Mitchell is mixed up in this thing, how do you know Huntley Banner wasn't the mastermind directing it all?"

"Because if he had been," Mason said, "there would have been no reason for Elvina to have taken all those chances in order to be in the office on Monday. She could have flown to Las Vegas right after she planted the bag in my office."

"And what about motive?" Judge Fallon asked.

"The motive," Mason said, "isn't as apparent as the identity of the killer. I'm not going to hazard a guess at this time. But once we get Miss Mitchell, I think we'll find the motive—and the motive may be rather complicated.

"I would like to have the police conduct a searching inquiry. I think Elvina Mitchell would crack wide open under interrogation."

Judge Fallon looked at Hamilton Burger.

The district attorney shook his head. "I still say this is just a runaround in order to plant suspicion so that it will take the pressure off the defendant.

"I don't try cases for the defendants," Hamilton Burger went on. "Perry Mason is fully capable of pointing out all those factors favoring the defendant—in fact he has done it very dramatically in this case. His reasoning is as fallacious as it is dramatic.

"He managed things so the bailiff would come running after Elvina Mitchell in a way that frightened the poor girl half to death. Even if she hadn't done a thing, the way Mason handled things she'd have started running."

Judge Fallon said, "I don't agree. I want Elvina Mitchell picked up. It shouldn't be difficult to apprehend her. The police can watch her apartment, they can watch the office, they can find where she parks her car, they can pick her up. When she is picked up I want her brought to me, and unless the district attorney is going to interrogate Minerva Hastings I want to talk with Lieutenant Tragg and instruct him to do it."

"Oh, very well," Hamilton Burger said wearily. "It's just another one of those run-arounds, but if Mason has convinced you he can convince the newspaper reporters, so I'll have to investigate that theory of the case."

"Please do so," Judge Fallon said, with cold formality, "and don't think this court is as credulous and naïve as your voice and manner seem to intimate."

SEVENTEEN

It was ten o'clock the next morning when Perry Mason, Hamilton Burger, Lt. Tragg and Adelle Hastings met in Judge Fallon's chambers in response to a judicial summons.

"I have asked you to be here," Judge Fallon said, "because I want to make certain that this case is so handled in open court that it protects the defendant without prejudicing the rights of other persons.

"As you people are, of course, aware, there is an estate involved here running to several million dollars. While I have become convinced in my own mind as to what happened, and I am assured that confessions have been obtained from some of the people, there will, nevertheless, have to be trials since the case is one involving first-degree murder.

"I have therefore asked Lieutenant Tragg to make a confidential statement, and I am asking that the defense refrain from turning over all the details of that statement to the press."

"As far as we're concerned," Mason said, "once the case against Adelle Hastings is dismissed, we have no further interest in the matter; except, of course, from a standpoint of property rights."

Judge Fallon said, "Huntley Banner is representing Minerva Hastings. I don't know what his attitude will be in regard to the civil litigation. However, Lieutenant Tragg can tell you of developments which took place early this morning, and which in justice to the district attorney, I should state, were communicated to me at his request, as soon as I answered the telephone this morning."

Judge Fallon nodded to Lt. Tragg. Tragg said tersely, without expression and very apparently measuring his words, "Helen Drexel is the daughter of Harley C. Drexel, a contractor in Carson City. Helen Drexel handled the business end of her father's operation during the summer vacation. Huntley Banner is Drexel's attorney.

"Drexel built a small house on the back of his lot, intending to rent it at what we would consider a rather exorbitant rental, to persons who were anxious to establish a six weeks' residence in Nevada for jurisdictional purposes.

"Because Helen Drexel had for a long time been a close friend of Elvina Mitchell, Banner's secretary, Miss Mitchell proceeded to supply clients who would occupy the house for the necessary period of time. One of those persons was Minerva Hastings, one of them was Rosalie Blackburn. They both became friendly with Helen Drexel, and both of them were friendly with Elvina Mitchell.

"Elvina Mitchell, in turn, is hopelessly head-over-heels in love with Connely Maynard, and for a long time felt that Maynard was not getting the business breaks he deserved from Garvin Hastings, that Simley Beason was gradually inspiring more confidence and being given more responsibilities.

"Minerva sympathized with Elvina Mitchell and one day put it up to her out of a clear sky that whenever Garvin Hastings died, Minerva would be the head of the business, that Connely Maynard would be given the position of chief executive and a share of the profits.

"What Minerva didn't know, and what Elvina hadn't known until a short time before, was that Connely Maynard had become involved financially and had embezzled money from the business. Simley Beason apparently either suspected this or was conducting some investigations which would soon give him the knowledge, and that, of course, would be fatal as far as Maynard was concerned.

"Apparently Minerva was not a party to the murder, but she did let Elvina know that she had a trump card in case anything should happen to Hastings before Hastings found out that she actually never had secured a divorce from him, and that his marriage to Adelle was legally bigamous.

"Elvina Mitchell shadowed Adelle Hastings that Sunday when she went to Ventura, found an opportunity to grab her bag off the seat of the automobile, had duplicate keys to Adelle's apartment made. She didn't need keys to the Hastings house because Connely Maynard knew where the key was kept in the office.

"After Adelle left the house Monday morning, Connely Maynard entered, killed Hastings in cold blood so that his defalcations would not be discovered, then ran to Elvina Mitchell to take the thing from there.

"Elvina put the fatal gun in Adelle's handbag, put on dark glasses and went to Mason's office during the noon hour. She gave the name of Adelle Hastings, planted the bag and then left.

"The next thing that bothered the conspirators was that Adelle might claim, with reason, the gun had been planted in her bag and her gun, being found in her apartment, would bear out the story. So Elvina chartered a plane to be in readiness just as soon as she could possibly get to the airport after leaving the office on Monday evening. She made a dash for Las Vegas, got there, as it happened, less than half an hour before Adelle arrived. She got into Adelle's house, stole Adelle's gun, and concealed it.

"The plot was all ready then to close the net on Adelle Hastings and frame her for murder."

"Just where does Banner fit into all this?" Mason asked.

"Banner's skirts are clean. At least we think they are," Tragg said.

"Yes, I can understand that if they hadn't been, if he had been a conspirator, Elvina could have taken the afternoon off to fly to Las Vegas and wouldn't have had to cut things so fine. As it was, she didn't want her employer to know anything about her activities, so she had to carry out her plot during the periods of freedom—the lunch hour and after the office closed."

"It seems," Lt. Tragg said, "that Hastings did execute a will in Adelle's favor after his marriage. He came to the office when Banner was out, told Elvina Mitchell what he wanted.

"Elvina told him that he could make a holographic will entirely in his own handwriting, date it and sign it, and it would be valid. Hastings did so and left the will with her.

"However, Banner is vulnerable to this extent. He knew, or had reason to believe, that such a will had been made. He thought that it had been lost from his files and apparently decided that he would say nothing about it. He didn't know that Elvina had deliberately destroyed that will.

"Now, as I understand it, once you prove the execution of the will, the fact that it was destroyed by third persons doesn't affect the validity of the will if you can prove it was once in existence."

Judge Fallon said, "That's right.

"Now then, I am going to go into court and call the case of the People of the State of California versus Adelle Hastings, and I take it you, Mr. Burger, will move to dismiss the case on the ground that the real culprit has been apprehended and has confessed."

Burger took a deep breath. "That is right," he said.

Adelle Hastings impulsively threw her arms around Mason's neck and kissed him.

Judge Fallon smiled. "I take it, then, we're ready to proceed as soon as Mr. Mason has removed the lipstick from his cheek."

THE END